The Sherman Letter

A Novel of History and Mystery

by
Leonard Palmer

A Write Way Publishing Book

Copyright© 1994 by Leonard Palmer

Write Way Publishing
3806 S. Fraser
Aurora, Colorado 80014

First Edition, 1995

ISBN 1-885173-08-3

0 1 2 3 4 5 6 7 8 9 10

Dedicated to my family
—Leonard Palmer
—1995

CHAPTER ONE

1865

The Captain watched the General sitting at his spartan desk, scribbling furiously. He coughed politely, one hand covering his mouth, the other clutching the cup of coffee he had brought for him.

The General turned at the sound. The terms of surrender and the troubles with Washington had taken their toll. His shock of reddish-brown hair was disheveled, and he looked like he had aged twenty years in the last few weeks. The hawkish face, piercing eyes, determined mouth and close-cropped beard affirmed the warrior in the man. But it was the deep-set wrinkles that betrayed the worry on his hardened face, as he stood on the threshold of total victory after four years of terrible war.

The Captain had served this General since 1861, the entire duration of the war. It was now early spring of 1865 and in all that time the Captain had only once gone back to his hometown on the southwest shore of Lake Michigan. Late at night, he sometimes lay in bed and thought of the lake; its thick rolling waves, the way the sun shone on it at dawn. It seemed a million miles away now. And a million years. Like the General, the Captain, too, looked older than his years.

Only twenty-two, he had seen hard action at Fort Donelson, Vicksburg, the madness that was Shiloh; then east with the General to Atlanta and the march through Georgia, where they left a landscape pockmarked with shell holes and dotted with thousands of fire-blackened chimneys; all that remained of the cities, farms, and factories they had put to the torch. Then they swung north through the Carolinas, here, to Raleigh. Lee had surrendered to Grant, and then Confederate General Johnston, with a much larger force, had surrendered to this man. Jeff Davis was rumored to be in flight to Kirby Smith's Texas. Lincoln was assassinated.

The insanity would soon be over. The Captain would be home soon, back to his brothers and sister and schoolteacher parents. He might as well have been told he was bound for the moon. There had been too many years, too many battles, too much hardtack, cold coffee, wormy bacon. Too much blood.

"Is that coffee for me, Stannie?" asked the General.

"Yes, sir," said the Captain. "I thought it might comfort you."

"It will, Stannie. Thank you." The General took the cup from the Captain and cupped it in his hands, guarding its warmth as he sipped the coal-black liquid. He smiled at the Captain. "Army coffee," he said, shaking his head.

"Yes, sir."

"Have you seen the papers that came today, Stannie?"

"Yes, sir. It's shameful."

"*The Chicago Tribune* called me insane."

"Yes, sir."

"*The New York Times* accused me of insubordination."

"Yes, sir."

"It's all Stanton's doing. I'm no politician. War is my business. Politicians are the worst kinds of snakes. I'd rather face the entire Army of Northern Virginia than one congressman in Washington."

"Yes, sir."

The General stood, stretched his lean, rawboned frame. "I'm going outside, Stannie, and take some air. I've had enough coffee, thank you. Leave the letter on the table. I'll post it later."

It was an order in the offhand way the General had with him. He wanted him to take the coffee away. After the General had left the room, the Captain walked up to the desk and picked up the coffee cup. It was uncharacteristic of him to read the General's correspondence, but he felt a compulsion to do so. As he bent over the desk and read the letter, it gradually filled him with a sense of urgency and fear. He had heard the General before, cursing Stanton and the newspapers as traitors and spies. He had known the General to be impetuous, to sometimes do things he later regretted. But *this*, he thought as he stared at the letter. But *this*.

The Captain picked up the letter, folded it and put it in his pocket. Then he took another piece of paper, quickly scribbled across its surface and spilled coffee over it so that the paper was drenched and unreadable. He picked up the soggy paper between thumb and forefinger and carried it onto the front porch, where he found the General smoking a long cigar and staring at the stars.

"General?" said the Captain.

"Yes, Stannie?"

"I'm afraid there's been an accident. I spilled coffee on your correspondence. It's totally ruined." He held up the dripping, coffee-soaked paper. The General glared and puffed furiously on his cigar. Its tip glowed like the fiery head of a comet. The Captain stared at his feet, fearing the worst.

"It's all right, Stannie," said the General after a moment. "Accidents will happen. I'll write another letter." As an afterthought, he said, "You didn't read it, did you?"

"The General's mail is not my business, sir."

The General grunted and dismissed him with a wave of his hand. The Captain retreated to his quarters, leaving William Tecumseh Sherman alone with his cigar and his thoughts. He may write another letter and post it, thought the Captain. But with luck, the General would think it over, as he sometimes did after his temper got the better of him, and the Captain would have prevented a crisis greater than Lincoln's assassination. In the privacy of his room, the Captain pulled the General's letter from his pocket and reread it. If the General ever found the letter on him, or in his room, he would have him shot. He undressed slowly, folded his clothes neatly and sank onto the bed. He dreamed of Lake Michigan, of his family playing in the waves. He was not part of the dream.

CHAPTER TWO

1991

Moon crouched on a bar stool at DiCiccio's saloon while a violent winter wind pummeled the plate glass windows and the factory city outside. He munched on a Milky Way, agonizing over the Gulf crisis playing itself out on the wide screen TV suspended from the tavern's tin ceiling. The world was marching to war, he thought, and everyone seemed to view it as the latest network miniseries.

"I'll have them turn that off, if it worries you so much," said Sally Andrews. Sally, who had once worked with Moon at the daily *Southport Times*, was sharing the better part of a snowy winter evening with him over friendly conversation and boilermakers.

"It drives me nuts, but I can't turn it off. Is everyone goofy, or what?" The screen flashed images of troops, marching in cadence, gun barrels flashing.

"There's been a lot of complaints about the media coverage," she said, watching in disapproval as he deposited the candy wrapper on the bar. "They say there's too much, and it could be pushing us into war."

"Hell, I *can't* believe that. When you're the top columnist for the top paper in your hometown, you're not supposed to knock the media." The screen flashed images of tanks—huge, lumbering things blasting cannon at thin air. He shuddered to think what their shells would do to flesh and bone.

"Top *weekly* paper," she said, reminding him he was no longer employed at the *Southport Times*. Sally had the condescending attitude toward weeklies that most daily newspaper people have—an attitude Moon had also held until *Times* publisher Charles Conrad, Jr., gave him the boot for insubordination and he went to work for the competing free weekly, *The Express*.

"And as far as this war goes, the rumor-mongers in the media are pushing everyone closer to war," she said.

"The people have a right to know all the facts," he said, quoting the time-honored journalists' credo. He chewed and swallowed the last of the Milky Way, eyeing her defiantly.

Her eyes, powder-blue like a fine pastel by Renoir, stared unbelievingly into his. "Please spare me that shop talk baloney," she said, "and it *is* baloney, Moon. You know it is."

The television was now focused on an "expert" analyst discussing the strength of the Iraqi army with the commentator. Bold type below described him as a retired army general. From what war? Moon wondered. He looked to be in his eighties.

He struck a superior pose. "Well, no matter what your jaded brain tells you, we journalists still have certain standards."

"That Woodward and Bernstein garbage won't wash with me. This is Southport, not Washington or New York." Without skipping a beat, she said, "You're not going to eat another one of those candy bars, are you?" She watched in disgust as he freed another Milky Way from its wrapper.

"I'm hungry. When I'm hungry, I eat what interests me."

"Eat a granola bar a day, like me. It's good for you."

He smoothed the wrinkles out of the green and brown

wrapper and held it up. "A Milky Way a day," he read, "helps you work, rest, and play."

"You're ruining your health," she said.

"I had a mom, you know, and she never bitched at me the way you do."

"That's another problem with you, Moon. You write like Byron, but sometimes you talk like a bleacher bum."

"A bleacher bum, maybe. But I've got my principles."

For Moon, life essentially boiled down to three basic rules. Number one: never owe money to a bank, they'll bust your chops and send you to the poorhouse if given half a chance. Second: don't put any faith in politicians, they're all whores who'll do anything to cut a deal and keep their jobs. Third: find and frequent a friendly neighborhood saloon where you can cash checks after banking hours and the owner will call a cab if you tie one on—a neighborhood saloon like DiCiccio's.

Since he'd moved from Chicago to Southport twenty years ago, DiCiccio's had become his favorite watering hole. A sports bar long before they came into vogue, it had anchored the corner of Milwaukee Avenue and Seventh Street in the factory city of 100,000 souls for over a century—a working class neighborhood of nondescript frame houses and neat postage stamp lawns. It had been a tavern all those years, with a succession of various oddball owners, except during the national insanity called Prohibition, when overnight it became a social club, a polite term for speakeasy. The walls were a crazy quilt of sports history: two signed photos of Jack Dempsey; a crossed pair of Bobby Hull's hockey sticks; poster-sized photos of Butkus and Nitzchke; hundreds of faded, curling snapshots of local high school and college sports heroes; and a large, musty moosehead caked with cobwebs and dust, rumored to have been shot by Teddy Roosevelt on one of his many western hunting trips.

Ralph DiCiccio, the current owner, hadn't trifled with the true spirit of the historic saloon, with the exception of adding a few photos of Italian-American NFL linemen on the walls. The previous owner, a hard-headed German named Franks, had adamantly refused to hang any new pictures unless they were muscle-bound Krauts. When Moon had questioned him about the huge photo of Jesse Owens he'd pinned to one wall, red-nosed Old Man Franks had said: "He iss Cherman, yah. He must be. He vass zo goot."

Ralph's greatest contribution to the old landmark was the Italian cooking of Mrs. Tempesta, a rotund Italian matron with a mustachioed upper lip and generous hips, who prepared just one item: skinny spaghetti with meatballs and sausage in a thick red sauce. The food drew crowds, mostly on weekends, but this snowy Saturday night had kept most of them snug in their homes, so when Sally and Moon retired from the bar they had no problem finding a booth in the barn-sized tavern. Ralph DiCiccio himself waited on them.

"I liked your last column, Moon," he said. "I just wonder how the mayor's gonna take it."

"He'll laugh, Ralph. He's got a good sense of humor."

"Show me a kraut who knows how to laugh ..." Ralph said, letting the sentence hang like a side of beef on a hook. He was lumping Mayor Milton Meyer and Old Man Franks together.

"Can we have two of the specials, please?" said Sally. "And make sure Moon gets an extra-big salad." She tossed Moon a reproachful look. "To make up for the candy you just poisoned your system with." Moon lifted his shoulders in a what-the-hell shrug.

"*Insalata grande*," Ralph said with a Mediterranean flourish of his hands. "I'll whip one up special myself, Moon." Like a grotesque lifted from a page of Leonardo's sketch book, Ralph had a huge nose and flushed cheeks. Bright white hair held down with too much hair tonic, floppy satellite dish ears and thick lips that looked like they'd been pasted on his face.

Within minutes, Ralph was back at the table with a basket

of crusty Italian bread and butter, a shaker of Romano cheese, a bowl of crushed red pepper, a small salad for Sally and a large bowl of healthy greens for Moon.

Moon speared a marble-sized, corpse-colored vegetable with his fork. "What's this?"

"A cicci bean. Garbanzo. Chick-pea. They're good for you."

"Which means they'll taste like shit." Moon popped the bean into his mouth. It had the taste and consistency of cardboard soaked in oil and left standing for a couple of months. He choked it down. "How about another couple beers?"

"Hey, Moon," said Sally as she stabbed at his hand with her fork. "Do you recognize her?" She nodded toward a fifty-something woman sitting at the bar, obviously working on a monumental drunk. Her spray-starched neon-blonde hair was piled high above her fleshy face. She wore black-rimmed glasses with lenses like twin glass-bottomed boats. Balanced precariously on her bar stool, she tossed a sidelong glance at them over a wicked-looking bluish drink.

"I don't recognize her," he replied, "but she seems to know us." The woman struggled off the stool and staggered toward their booth.

"Oh, oh," he said. "Here she comes." By the time he'd finished the sentence, the woman had plunked herself down and slid in next to Moon, setting her glass on the table with the focused care of an experienced drunk. Up close, the drink looked like some ancient alchemist's concoction.

"See your column every week, 'cept you don't look anything like your picture." She pronounced picture something like pissure. Her breath smelled of unidentifiable booze.

"Thanks," he said. "I hope you like it."

"Hate it." She gulped the dregs of her drink and slammed the glass on the table. "It's bullshit, pure an' simple. Pap for the rabble."

"'Pap for the rabble'? Wasn't that some San Francisco punk rock group?" Moon replied to the drunk. Her eyes were glazed donuts of incomprehension. "Never waste witty remarks on the inebriated," Moon said as Sally squirmed uncomfortably in her seat.

"Ms. Haskell," Sally said as the woman swayed before them. "I enjoyed your books very much."

"Miz Haskell? Do I know you?"

Sally obviously regretted she'd opened her mouth. "Not really," she said.

"Tha's right." Haskell stared into her empty glass. "Need 'nother drink," she mumbled as she rose unsteadily and slogged back to her stool.

"Charming woman. Who is she?" Moon asked.

"That was Elaine Haskell." Sally said it as if he was an idiot for not recognizing the woman.

"Who the hell is Elaine Haskell?"

"She's written several important books on Southport history. She's recognized as an expert."

"Well, she's definitely not an expert on what to drink or how much. That lady has a Brobdingnagian snootful. And did you catch that drink? It looked like something out of a nineteen thirty's Flash Gordon flick."

"She's a creative genius," said Sally in her defense. "She's entitled to let off a little steam once in a while."

"I wish you could reason away my little shortfalls with such brilliant logic."

"If you want to kill yourself boozing, that's your business."

"Tell me true, Sally, has cupid let loose his bolt? Are you finally falling in love with me?"

"Hardly. I just don't want to see you waste your talent with booze, that's all."

"Like your creative genius there at the bar?" He nodded at Elaine Haskell, who was downing a fresh baby-blue drink. She threw back her head, drained the glass, rocked off the stool, and landed flat on her back with a loud thud like a raw

T-bone slapped against the floor, glasses flying off her face. Ralph rushed from behind the bar and grabbed her by the armpits in an attempt to help her stand, accidentally stepping on her glasses and breaking them. She didn't need them anyway. She was out cold.

"Jesus," Ralph said to no one in particular as he stared at the inert woman. "I'm sorry. I didn't realize she was that far gone."

"That's okay, Ralph," Moon shouted back in support. "You don't need to make excuses for short hitters."

A squat guy at the bar with a simian brow and Butkus-sized shoulders thrust his beer gut in Moon's direction. "Why don't you shuddup?" he growled.

Moon rose deliberately from the booth. Sally tugged at his sleeve. "Don't start anything, Moon," she said. "Did you see his meat hooks? He'll rip your head off. He's just looking for an excuse to clobber somebody."

"I didn't start anything. He did." He stepped over the comatose Elaine Haskell and butted up against the gorilla, who pushed his rock-hard paunch, stretched tight as a drum, into Moon's stomach.

"What did you say?" Moon said.

"I said for you to shuddup."

Moon stretched his six-five frame to its fullest, towering a good six inches over him. Ralph DiCiccio dropped Elaine Haskell when he saw the confrontation, her head cracking against the floor like a rifle shot. He quickly moved toward the two combatants, but Moon had already cocked a fist and readied to fire. The gorilla was a split second faster, putting one solid uppercut smack under his chin. Moon's teeth snapped together with a sharp click, and just before he dropped into dreamland, he heard Ralph say "Oh, shit," and Sally moan "Not again." He slumped down on the floor, cheek to cheek with the drunken historian.

CHAPTER THREE

A rough knock on Sally's apartment door jerked Moon out of dreamland. He was nursing one hell of a headache—from too much liquor and a rock-hard fist to the jaw. His head was propped on three fat pillows on Sally's sofa, where he'd spent the night.

"Who is it, Sal?" he asked as she hurried out of her bedroom and picked her way through his scattered clothes to the door.

"Oh, Christ," Moon complained as Detective Manny Edison of the Southport PD filled the doorway. He strolled in uninvited as Sally stared at him quizzically.

"Who in the heck are you?" she demanded while attempting to block his path. The cop gave her an impolite shove and strode by her.

You'd have to take off your shoes and socks to count the nicknames Emmanuel Edison had picked up over the years. In his first years on the force in the Sixties he'd acquired the sobriquet "Hippie," because of his bushy red hair and beard, or sometimes "Bozo" because of the way his hair stood out at the sides of his head. He made his name then as the premium hard-guy buster of drug dealers even though most of the unfortunates he sent up to Green Bay or Taycheedah in those early days of the drug era were small-timers, twenty-year-old kids selling a kilo of Mexican grass or brick of hash.

As the drug industry matured and became increasingly violent, Manny picked up new tags—"Slither" and "Snake" in the early 1970s, then "Luke Skywalker" for awhile at the end of the decade, when he had dropped on Southport a load of pure windowpane acid—busting a few dealers and making a few extra bucks for himself. Then, as the Seventies slid into the Eighties, Manny Edison became the Rambo of the streets. He dropped all pretense of undercover narcotics and began to wear ankle-length leather coats and crazy hats that reflected his mood. A homburg or fedora meant you could count on a rational Manny Edison, but if you ran afoul of him when he sported a baseball cap with the long brim that buried his rat's eyes in its shadow, you were in big trouble. Today the renegade cop was hatless, his once-abundant red mop slicked down in a vain effort to hide his balding crown.

In 1985, Manny had garnered his current nickname, "Son of Sam," or as he was known in Southport's small but growing ghetto, "Son of Sam Motherfucker," because he carried a .44 Smith and Wesson that he occasionally shot people with, but more often used Wyatt Earp style, clubbing his suspects into the ground until they nearly bled to death or confessed. Manny was the last, bitter fruit from the twisted reign of the late Chief Chester LeBlanc, and he managed to keep his job because, like J. Edgar Hoover, he had too much shit on too many people. But he had been relegated to ghetto detail, lording it over the drunks, junks and punks, making small-time deals and small-time busts.

"You seen this?" he said, tossing the morning's edition of the *Chicago Tribune* on Moon's lap. He restlessly tapped a skinny finger on the side of his hooked nose. A long white scar ran

across his right cheek, where a bullet had creased him during
a violent shoot-out between two local pimps and Edison and
his then-partner Whistler Evans. Evans and Edison had been
shaking down the pimps, putting the screws to them so tightly
that the pimps decided to waste them one broiling summer
night, lying in ambush for them in a stretch of bushes on a
dark side street parallel to the Chicago and North western
elevated tracks. The pimps, both packing Colt Python .357
magnums, opened up on the cops as they approached an abandoned home for a supposed pay-off. The first shot from the
pimps' pistols caught Whistler Evans smack in the chest,
knocking him back five feet and into the street, dead before
he hit the concrete. The third shot creased Edison's cheek,
leaving a bloody trail of fire that had healed into the white
scar he now wore as a badge. The cop dropped, yanked out
his .44 and pumped five shots into the bushes, where he had
seen the muzzle flashes from the pimps' guns. His second
shot blew a four inch hole in the face of one pimp. His fourth
tore a chunk out of the shoulder of the second, who leaped
out of the cover of the bushes and raced down the side street,
Edison in hot pursuit.

The pimp made it down the long stretch of neglected
street, past three homes whose owners wisely kept their shades
drawn and curtains pulled tight. At the end of the block, under a street light that illuminated him like a stage spotlight,
the pimp stopped, wheeled and got off one wild shot at the
cop. The bullet careened off the concrete abutment of the elevated tracks, whining as it chipped concrete and sparks off
the graffiti-sprayed wall. Edison snapped off his last shot at
the pimp and blew away the top of his skull along with his
purple wide-brimmed hat.

Edison got a police commendation and William "Whistler" Evans got a magnificent funeral, at which Edison delivered his partner's eulogy and police from Southport, Mil-

waukee and Chicago attended as mourners.

Moon stared at the newsprint. "Seen what?"

"Page ten. Check it out. Mind if I smoke?" He pulled a pack of Lucky Strikes from his shirt pocket and fired one up without waiting for an answer.

Moon displayed the article with its grainy photograph to Sally. "Jesus, Sal, isn't this the old broad who was at Ralph's last night?"

"Don't say 'broad,'" she admonished as she stared at the photograph under the headline. "My God! It is!"

Moon read the story aloud: "Prominent historian freezes to death. Elaine Haskell, fifty-three, Executive Director of the Southport Historical Society, was found frozen to death in the front yard of her home in exclusive Smithdale late last night.

"Ms. Haskell was the author of several books on Southport and Wisconsin history, including a Civil War treatise on the commitment of Southport soldiers, that was highly praised by history scholars.

"Ms. Haskell allegedly was drinking in a Southport tavern last night before taking a taxi home, and Southport police are in the process of questioning tavern patrons.

"Ms. Haskell leaves no relatives. Funeral arrangements are being handled by the Southport Historical Society."

Moon handed the paper back to Manny. "So what's this got to do with us?"

Manny continued restlessly tapping his nose, a Morse code only he could understand. "My nose tells me you were in Ralph's last night. I'm checking out the facts, talking to witnesses."

"The paper said she froze. Accidental death."

"You never know, Mr. Writer, what an autopsy will turn up. She sat in your booth. Did she talk about anything unusual?"

"Like what?"

"Like maybe some letters she'd lost?"

"What letters?"

Manny shook a cautionary finger, and Moon could see the ominous bulge of his .44 in its shoulder holster. "I'm the one asking the questions."

"She was so drunk she couldn't string two sentences together, let alone talk about any missing letters. Was she writing you love letters and you want to get them back before somebody goes public?"

A wicked grin split Manny's face. "Heard you got your clock cleaned last night. Again."

"The guy hit me when I wasn't looking."

"How's it down at that little paper you're working on now? Good to see your career moving along at such a fast clip."

"I get along. How's the drug and money-laundering business?"

"I make more in a week than you do in a year. By the way, I slept with your ex last night. She's a great piece of ass."

Manny blew a thick cloud of smoke at Moon. Moon flagged Edison's noxious fumes from his face. "Good for you. You two deserve each other. What are you doing on legitimate police work anyway?"

"Impolite, Moon," he said, rolling up the newspaper and shoving it under his arm. "Always impolite." As he stopped at the open doorway he reminded Moon of Lon Chaney in *The Phantom of the Opera*—hollow eyes, skin like a yellowed lamp shade with a weak bulb shining through.

"I know you, Moon," said the cop. "You're a nosy bastard. You just forget what we talked about just now. It's none of your business." He exited, trailing acrid smoke and suspicion in his wake.

"Who was that?" asked Sally incredulously. "What a creep."

"Manny Edison of the Southport PD, aka Scumbag."

"That was a terrible thing he said about your wife. He hates your guts, doesn't he?"

"Feeling's mutual, but you know, a guy like that can smell a rat a mile away. He thinks something stinks, it usually does. Too bad about your hero, though, drunk and stuck to the sidewalk."

"She wasn't my hero. And don't get sarcastic, Truman."

She'd used his first name. She knew Moon detested the name and used it to needle him.

"Why did Manny come to me?" he asked. "There were other customers at Ralph's last night."

"What did he mean by saying you never know what an autopsy would reveal? He makes me nervous."

Sally was right to be nervous, he thought. What *did* the creep want? And what in the hell did he mean by 'lost letters'?

All of it made Moon feel damned uncomfortable.

CHAPTER FOUR

1865

A bony hand clamped over Stanford Short's mouth as he slept in his comfortable bed, dreaming of Lake Michigan. He awoke with a start and struggled to sit up, but the hand pressed down harder, stifling his angry yell. A harsh voice whispered into his ear. "You jes' hush!"

Even in the pitch black, Short knew whose hand was clamped over his mouth. He could tell by the smell. It was Meriwether Pickens, steward in Sherman's headquarters. Pickens was also from Southport, where members of his family were well-known ne'er-do-wells. Meriwether Pickens' sense of loyalty to the cause was suspect at best. He had skulked at the battle of Shiloh, not moving into the front lines until a lieutenant of the Fourth Illinois had threatened him with his saber. Pickens had somehow managed to finagle his way into becoming a steward in Sherman's headquarters, and Short thought it disgusting, the way Pickens groveled at the General's feet. Short would have liked nothing better than to see Pickens put back into the front lines to face Confederate shot and shell.

"Christ," muttered Short as Pickens removed his hand from

Short's mouth. "What do you want, Pickens?"

The full stench from the soldier's filthy clothes and body rose to violate his nose. Adjusting his eyes to the dark, Short could see Pickens' stubble of beard, sunken eyes, sharp nose. The effect was of an oversized vulture's mask.

Pickens made a sour face, pinching his lips together. "Oh, yes," he said. "Mr. High and Mighty now that you gone an' been made a captain. Jes' don't you ferget: I know you. I know yer family, too." Short recognized this as a threat. Pickens' remaining brothers and sisters were back in Southport, in close contact with Short's family.

Pickens leaned over and put his mouth close to Short's ear. "Where is it, Short?"

"Where is what?" Short said impatiently. He would have called for the guard to toss Pickens out, if it weren't for the thinly veiled threat he had made against his family.

"The letter," said Pickens. "The letter you stole off'n the General's table."

Short's pulse begin to race. How in the hell did Pickens know about the letter? He spoke slowly, controlling his voice. "What letter?"

"Goddam you, Short! You know what goddam letter I mean."

"No, I don't know what you mean." Short was beginning to lose his temper.

"I was there. Afore you come, the General left the room, an' I snuck in. I seed the letter on th' table. I read some of it. Then th' General come back an' I hid in th' closet. I seed you steal it. I want that letter."

"You can't have it," said Short, pushing the man and his stench away.

"I know a coupla newspapers that'd gimme a hefty price to get their hands on it." Suddenly conciliatory, he added, "How 'bout it, Short? You gimme the letter, an' we split the money. You kin be a rich man."

"The General never meant to post the letter," said Short. "If it fell into the wrong hands, it could mean extending this war. Many thousands more could be killed. The General would be disgraced."

"The devil with him!" said Pickens, making a fist and raising his voice, casting his eyes around to see if anyone had heard. "That letter means money fer me, boy." He emphasized the "boy." Short was five years his junior, and it rankled him. "You git me that letter, boy, an' we kin do business." Meriwether Pickens slunk out of the room, garbage scent trailing behind him like an obedient shadow.

Short lay back on his bed and stared at the ceiling. He would post the envelope with Sherman's letter tomorrow. And then he would have to deal with Pickens before Pickens dealt with him.

"No more blood, goddam it," he groaned. "No more war, Pickens."

He continued to stared at the ceiling, unable to sleep. His sheets were soaked with sweat.

CHAPTER FIVE

1991

"Funny thing is," Ralph said. "The cabbie took her home. Says he walked her into the house and everything. Says she fell right onto her living room couch and passed out. How she got back outside is a real mystery."

"Cops know this?" asked Moon.

"Sure. But they figure that she must've gotten up some time in the night and wandered outside. Fell down. Hit her head or something."

"They question the cabbie?"

"Yup. And he told 'em everything. Too bad. They said she was a famous person."

"She wrote books," said Sally, dumping a level teaspoon of powdered non-dairy creamer into a glass cup of Ralph's tepid coffee. Moon nursed a tap beer, waiting for the Bears-Giants playoff on Ralph's wide-screen. "She was an expert on the Civil War."

"I was in WW Two myself." He bore down on the Ws. "The Big One." A group of Packer fans at one end of the bar hollered for drinks. It was nearing game time, and they wanted to be properly fueled to root for their team as they cracked helmets against the Bears. They wore green and yellow Green Bay sweatshirts and stocking caps. Most of them were unshaven and all of them had beer bellies.

"Listen to them," Moon said disgustedly. "Living in the past. Lombardi's been dead for twenty years."

"Sorry, but they're customers," said Ralph. "Gotta go. And if you want to talk to the cabbie who took her home last night, he's sitting there."

"Where?"

Ralph aimed a finger at a scrawny figure with a battered snap-tab cap sitting at the far corner of the bar, hunched over his beer like a dog guarding his dinner.

"Might make a good story, Moon," said Ralph over his shoulder, hustling to the Packer fans, now pounding on the bar.

"I'm on vacation," Moon said as the barkeep hurried away. He turned to Sally.

"What do you think?"

"It's up to you, Moon. I thought you wanted to watch the game. And you really *are* on vacation."

"A couple questions won't hurt." He grabbed his beer and headed for the end of the bar.

The cabbie's name was Mark Keith and yes, he said, he'd have a beer on Moon. He was a shade under six feet tall, with a body like a weathered fence post and a big nose reminiscent of a church key. Ralph's son Steve, assisting his old man on this busy football Sunday, set them up two beers. Crowd noise blasting from the television signalled kick-off time. The Packer fans, hell-bent for a monumental drunk, started cheering for the Giants.

"You like football?" Moon asked.

The wide brim of his old cap, flattened by the years, carved deep shadows in his face. "I like the Cubs," he said. "Football, I can take it or leave it." He turned his head, stiff-necked like a robin ogling a worm on the lawn, to get a better angle at Moon. "I know you. I seen you before. You write for the paper, right?"

"Right. *The Express.*"

"And I bet you want to ask me about last night, right? About the old lady?"

"Bingo."

"You gonna do a story on her?"

"I don't exactly do stories. I'm not a real journalist. I only write opinion."

"You gonna comment on this?"

"I'm on vacation."

"After vacation?"

"Let's just say I'm a nosy guy. It goes with the territory."

Mark Keith grinned, revealing tartar-caked teeth. "Well, okay then, nosy guy. But let me tell you, this lady was one hell of a ride."

"How do you mean?"

"I had to fight to get her into the cab. And then she wouldn't give me her address, and I hadda come back inside to get it from Ralph. He got it from the phone book. All the way home, she's yelling and screaming at me. Real foul stuff, too. Then I gotta fight to get her out of the cab and into her house. When we got inside, that's when it got *real* strange."

"How do you mean, 'strange?'" Moon flagged Steve DiCiccio for two more beers.

"She says for me to wait a minute, she's got to go into another room to get me some money, and she disappears. So I wait around a coupla minutes twiddlin' my thumbs. I look around a little. She's got a real nice house. Lot better than my efficiency."

"She pay you?"

"Listen, buddy. She came out of her bedroom stark-naked! Not a stitch on. Nowhere! And I mean she was *old*. And ugly! All wrinkled. I about blew my lunch."

Moon wondered what his current girl friends looked like. He wasn't exactly Robert Redford himself. "You mean she made a pass?"

"A pass? I'd call some old broad strippin' down to her birthday suit and grabbin' for my crotch more than a pass, wouldn't you?"

"Well, what did you do?"

"I told her I had a girlfriend, but that didn't stop her. She kept sayin' that I could stay the night, she'd work off what she owed me for the cab ride. I told her she'd have to pay me more if she wanted me to jump her bones."

"How'd she react to that?"

"She got real insulted. Never tell a broad you don't want to screw 'em. Not even some eighty-year-old gramma, like this one was. She started swingin' at me, so I put up my hands t' defend myself." He made two ineffectual fists with his bony hands.

"You probably don't believe me," he said. "But I can take care of myself pretty good."

He was right. Moon probably didn't believe him. "Then what happened?"

"I give her one small shot. Right here." He tapped himself sharply under the chin. "She went down like a ton of bricks. I tell you, sometimes I don't even know my own strength," he boasted, as if knocking out a fifty-year-old drunken woman was something to be proud of.

"What did you do then?"

"I picked her up, laid her out on the couch, and got the hell out of there. Didn't even get my cab fare." His Adam's apple bobbed as he guzzled a long drink of beer. "I tell you, Mister. This is a weird business. I could tell you stories."

"I believe it," Moon said. "So she was naked and out cold on her couch when you left her?"

"Just like I said: out like a light."

"Did you tell the cops all of this?"

"Everything. We all had a laugh about it, too."

"I bet. Did she say anything to you about some letters?"

"Huh?"

"Forget it." Moon shook his hand. It was like gripping a bent beer can. "Thanks."

"Thanks for the beers. So, you gonna write about this?"

"I doubt it. It's a little too risqué for a family newspaper."

"Riss-kay?" he said, squinting a bloodshot eye. "Oh, yeah. I see what you mean."

Moon slid back down the bar and repeated the cabbie's story to Sally.

She shook an angry fist under his nose. "Don't say it, Moon. Just keep your big mouth shut." She'd put Elaine Haskell on a pedestal, and the old gal had tumbled off.

Moon thought about the historian, staggering in front of their booth the night before. "Brilliant, drunk and horny," he mumbled softly so Sally couldn't hear. "A hell of a combination."

One of the Packer fans belched like a foghorn as the Bears fumbled the ball a yard short of the goal line. His buddies laughed and pounded on the bar for another round.

CHAPTER SIX

1865

Pickens followed Short everywhere the next morning, keeping a good distance behind, but always there. Short would jerk his head around and see Pickens' head quickly slide behind a corner, or the tail of his filthy blue coat disappear around a tree trunk.

At first Short had made up his mind to destroy the letter and settle the Meriwether Pickens problem once and for all, but something inside him told him not to do it. It was probably the memory of his schoolteacher father's lessons. "The artifacts of history," his father had said in his usual loving but pompous manner, "are as priceless as diamonds or emeralds. Those who callously destroy them are no better than thieves or murderers, for they are depriving future generations of their understanding of the past."

Because Stanford Short had taken his father's words to heart, he put away the idea of destroying the letter. As damning as it was, the letter was still a significant piece of history, although it would take other generations to fathom that significance. Short really didn't know if he wanted future generations to see his beloved General's indiscretions. At the same time, he didn't want to see the letter destroyed. The only solution was to send the letter to his father.

Short penned a terse note and sealed it, along with the

envelope containing Sherman's letter, into another envelope. He did not give it to the orderly to post, because the orderly could have easily been coerced by Meriwether Pickens into giving him Short's mail. A few dollars would have accomplished the task. Short held the mail on his own person until he handed it to a special post rider himself, keeping man and horse in sight until they disappeared. He walked back down the road to headquarters. In the front yard, he came face to face with Meriwether Pickens who smiled, revealing teeth stained from chewing tobacco.

"I sure hope you ain't done nothin' foolish Short," he said. He had his hands in his pockets, spit a long brown stream of tobacco dangerously close to Short's polished boot.

"You are supposed to salute when you pass a superior officer, private," said Short.

"Well, you see one, sonny, you jes' point'm out, y'hear?" replied Pickens, maintaining his smart-ass grin. Short raised an arm and motioned to a corporal wandering past.

"Corporal!" he commanded. The corporal stopped in his tracks. "Come here," ordered Short.

The corporal double-timed it over to the captain and stood at attention. "Sir!" he said.

Short pointed to Pickens, who still hadn't saluted or come to attention. "This man is on report for insubordination," said Short to the corporal. "I want you to escort him to the guard house."

"Yes, sir!" said the corporal, grabbing Pickens by the collar. The scruffy man jerked away, grinning at Short.

"Easy time," he said to Short. "Few days in the guard house'll do wonders fer my constitution." He stuck his nose in Short's face. Short shut his eyes as the smell hit him. Even outdoors, the man smelled like a pig pen.

"Jes' you remember," Pickens warned, "not t' do nothin' t' that letter ...Captain," he added sarcastically.

The corporal yanked Pickens' collar. "Come on, you." He led him away to the guard house as Pickens looked back at Short one more time, grinning devilishly.

CHAPTER SEVEN

1991

Monday. A cold, brittle day. First day of Moon's vacation. He always took two weeks in the dead of winter, when he could hunker down through the worst of what he called "Ma Nature's temper tantrums." He burrowed deeper under the covers as the room buzzer, sounding like an angry mutant wasp, announced a phone call in the hotel lobby. He threw a pillow at the buzzer, then a shoe. It continued rasping. Finally, cursing, he pulled on pants and shirt, skipped the shoes and socks and ran downstairs barefoot.

"Moon?" It was Sally on the line.

"Hey. I'm on vacation, remember?" He rubbed crusty sleep from his eyes, checked the hotel lobby clock. 10 AM. Almost dawn.

"Sorry to disturb your beauty sleep, but I thought you'd be interested in the story they're stripping in for tonight's edition."

"What story?"

"The police have arrested that cabby you talked to yesterday. Mark Keith."

"Arrested him for what?"

"Elaine Haskell's murder. He confessed."

"Confessed? Murder? You're sure?"

"That's what the story says, Moon. Gotta go. Bye." The line went dead.

This was a kick in the fanny, thought Moon. If the cops had enough evidence to claim Elaine Haskell was murdered, then the cabbie was tailor-made to take the fall. He couldn't figure the confession. Had the cabbie lied to him? With nothing better to do, he decided to check it out.

★★★

Deputy Assistant Medical Examiner Sylvia Smith arched a suspicious eyebrow, as one lock of silver hair worked its way out of her carefully arranged hairdo and stood, rebellious. She smacked at it unsuccessfully and it continued to spring up—a bright sliver, mutinous jack-in-the-box.

"George isn't here," she said, referring to her boss, George Beasley. "And this area is restricted." She looked around, as if her absent superior would suddenly appear and rescue her.

Moon tried to edge his way past her bulk blocking the doorway into the examiner's room, where all city autopsies were performed. "Big news story, Sylvia," he said.

"George isn't here," Sylvia repeated, firmly entrenched in the doorway. As he watched Sylvia defend her space, a line from a high school history book flashed through his mind— 'they shall not pass' — from some forgotten war in some forgotten place.

"Some information, then."

She stood at ease and swiped at her unruly lock of hair. "What?" she asked suspiciously.

"The old lady they brought in last night. Elaine Haskell. How did she die?"

"You'll have to get that from the police."

"They've arrested an innocent man for her murder."

"How do you know that?"

"I know the man. He couldn't have committed murder."

★★★

"Then he'll be all right, won't he?"

"Where's your boss?"

"He's out of town at a seminar. He won't be back until tomorrow." She smiled, self-satisfied. In command.

"Look. I'm asking you for a favor. To help an innocent man."

"No way. Never."

Her intransigence forced him to try another tack. He recalled that her boss was an avid horse player, constantly in debt to bookies and loan sharking juice men. "George still playing the ponies? I can have a few bookie friends call in your boss' markers. Maybe you can perform the autopsy after they get through with him."

"That's shitty, Moon. That's not playing by the rules. You wouldn't do that."

"Try me."

She eyeballed him angrily. "The first indication was that she froze. There was a circumorbital haematoma."

"A what?"

"A black eye. My first impression was that it could have happened when she fell. But there was something wrong about it, though. It didn't seem to fit. And I was right. When I examined her, I noticed a small bruise on the back of her head. Right here." She fingered a spot behind her right ear.

"She could've gotten that in a drunken fall, too," said Moon.

She shook her head and the rebellious silver lock shimmied obscenely. "No. It was made by some sort of a blunt object. Deliberately."

"Like what?"

"I couldn't really think of anything that small and round,

except for a ballpeen hammer."

"A hammer?"

"Or something with that type of surface. But whatever it was, it was done deliberately. My guess is that she was sleeping, or passed out and somebody rolled her over, pulled her hair up, and banged her in the back of the head. Then he let her hair back down to cover where she'd been hit."

"Did the blow kill her?"

"No. She froze to death."

"Was she clothed when she was found?"

"What do you mean?"

"I mean, was she naked?"

"Of course not!" Her tone was indignant.

"That's odd."

"What's so odd about having your clothes on?"

"Has Manny Edison been nosing around, asking questions?"

"Detective Edison was here, yes. Why?"

"Did he ask anything about any letters?"

"What letters?" Her blank stare told Moon she wasn't lying.

"Nothing. I owe you one, Sylvia."

"I didn't do it for you. I did it for George." She slapped down the unruly curl and held it firmly in place with her hand. "But don't tell anyone I told you," she warned.

Moon made a zipping motion with finger and thumb across his lips. "My lips are sealed," he said.

"And Moon ..."

"What?"

"I won't forget you threatened George, you bastard."

"Goodbye, Sylvia." He left her to the stench of formaldehyde and refrigerated corpses.

Moon stood outside the Rambler in the hospital parking lot, stroking his chin. Elaine Haskell had been hit on the head and dragged outside, where she was discovered fully dressed. But Mark Keith had said he'd left her stark-naked. Manny Edison had smelled a rat *before* the cabbie had been arrested. Something didn't jibe. Maybe a visit to the Southport Historical Society would be useful.

CHAPTER EIGHT

Moon had won the car ten years before: a 1965 Rambler Classic 770 convertible: clean lines, a fantastic 232 horsepower big six engine, robin's egg blue factory finish, simple chrome trim with a white naugahyde interior and a white rag in an all-night poker game, where he put up his marker for $1,000 against the car. His spades straight flush shot down a street-wise bookie named Hippo who regularly downed a case of Pepsi and two dozen jelly donuts during marathon poker fests.

A great set of wheels for summertime cruising with the top down, the Rambler was out of its element in the winter. Like many vintage rags, it was drafty, and he had to keep an eye out for road salt on the rocker panels and wheel wells.

Snow descended in fat, sloppy flakes, and the Rambler's worn-out wipers smeared them around its dingy windshield. Moon cursed as the car hopped the curb in front of the Historical Society. To add injury to insult, he slipped and fell on the icy sidewalk, banging his elbow sharply on the frozen concrete. Pain shot up his arm like he'd stuck his finger in a light socket.

The Southport Historical Society was housed in a quirky turn-of-the-century Queen Anne mansion in Civic Center Park in what used to be the hub of the city's business district. The thirty-room mansion, an ornate architectural wedding cake, was built by a wealthy brewer in the days when Southport was home to three breweries cranking out suds around the clock for the thirsty men who toiled in the city's dungeon-like factories. The home was a funeral parlor for ten years after the brewer died and then sat vacant for another five years until the Historical Society, flush with a large endowment from a local industrialist and a matching county grant, bought the building and moved their offices, displays, and archives to the new location. In the early 1970s, a tasteful addition had been added to the back end of the building, to accommodate the ever growing demands on the Society.

As he stood at the front door, Moon balanced on one leg like a flamingo, brushed snow off his pants and cursed the bad weather, the wipers on his car, the ice-covered sidewalk and life in general. Finally, a wizened female face popped up in the beveled window set into the oversized intricately-carved walnut door. He straightened up and smiled. The face didn't smile back.

Moon winced as he extended his arm. It felt like he had damn near busted his elbow. "Can I come in?"

"We're closed," mouthed the face.

"I hurt my elbow," he said, appealing to her maternal instincts. Moon held up his arm for her to see.

She opened the door. "I'm sorry," she said. "I didn't know you were hurt."

He stepped into a grand front parlor. A sweeping double staircase that led up to a large mezzanine and a bank of bay windows took his breath away. The walls were covered with faded photos of Southport and oil paintings of what he assumed were long-dead local dignitaries. Combined with a prominent musty odor, the effect was that of homey solidity.

"Can I get you something for your elbow?" As tiny as you

can get without being labeled a midget, the elderly woman spoke in a cracked soprano. Wearing a high-collared dress with ruffles on the sleeves, her hair pulled back into a neat Victorian bun, she seemed as much a part of the decor as the furniture and pictures. "I'm Tessie Allen," she said.

"Moon."

"Moon what?"

"Just Moon, thanks." A painful tingling chewed its way into his elbow as hot, healing blood rushed in.

"We're closed, you know," she said. "Do you need a bandage or something, for your arm?"

"No, thank you. Do you work here?"

"I'm a docent. A volunteer. I was doing some research in the archives when you rang the bell." She looked impatiently at the staircase as though she wanted to bolt and run up it.

"Did you know Elaine Haskell?" he asked abruptly.

"Are you from the police? They were here earlier today."

"Skinny guy with red hair? Long leather coat?"

"Yes."

"He's the cop. I'm from the newspaper."

She cocked her head the way a puppy does when it's trying to understand what you're saying. She held up a delicate finger. He thought he saw light through her parchment-like flesh. "You write the column ...?"

"Page three. Yeah, that's me."

She seemed to relax after recognizing Moon. He realized that newspaper people have an easier time with seniors, that they are the bulk of newspaper readership, even free weeklies like *The Express*; although management didn't like to admit it, spending the last ten years trying to pretend they're TV, with all sorts of gimmicks to lure kids into their pages—expanded comics, puzzles, music video reviews and worse. Cluttering up an adult product with kiddie news that has no relevance to its real readers.

In a hopeful tone, she asked. "Are you going to do a story on Elaine?"

Moon began to tell her he was on vacation, just nosing around, but he knew he'd get a better response if he hinted that he was going to eulogize her dead boss in his next column. "A great lady," he replied. And a monumental drunk, he thought.

"Yes," she said nodding her head slowly, as if with great effort. "A terrible, terrible tragedy. How she could have slipped in the snow— well, it's just tragic."

It dawned on him that she hadn't been informed of Mark Keith's arrest. "Was she working on something important? Some new research?"

"Oh, yes, Mr. Moon, she was." She looked hesitantly back up the steps.

"I'm not supposed to allow visitors into the archives on closed days, but seeing it's you ..." She crooked her finger and he followed her up the wide steps to the mezzanine and through a small door leading to the new addition and the archives. He faced long rows of dusty tomes and dog-eared maps on the walls.

A balding, effeminate man sat at one of the research tables. He wore a pair of round spectacles that were much too large for him, looking like a baby when he grabs daddy's glasses and puts them on his own face. He examined Moon with obvious distaste and glanced at Tessie Allen while he nudged his glasses back up on the bridge of his nose. Moon fought the urge to reach across the table and slap the spectacles off his face.

"Mr. Owen, this is Mr. Moon," Tessie said nervously. It was obvious that Mr. Owen was the rooster (or maybe the capon, thought Moon) that ruled this hen house. "He writes the column for the newspaper."

Owen continued to coldly stare over the tops of his glasses.

He didn't smile or offer to shake hands. "I know. I recognize him. What does he want?"

"I'm looking into Elaine Haskell's death," Moon said. "I was told she was doing some important research." Mr. Owen flashed his laser-beam stare at Miss Allen. A hot flush crept up over her high collar.

"How did you know about Elaine's research, then?" he asked sarcastically.

"She told me about it the other night."

"In a *bar*, I suppose? Dead drunk?" Elaine Haskell's drinking was obviously a poorly-kept secret.

"Not dead drunk. Talkative."

"I certainly believe that. But I'm sorry, we can't help you. Elaine's research project is in abeyance. Perhaps in a couple of weeks, after we get things sorted out, we might be able assist you." He rudely poked his nose back into the book.

After Owen's curt dismissal, Tessie Allen walked Moon back to the front door. "I'm sorry," she said.

Moon watched fat snowflakes blanket his car. He'd have to stop at a parts store for new wipers if he was going negotiate winter without a fatal accident. "Is there anyone else working here that I can talk to about Elaine?"

"No. Elaine was Executive Director. Mr. Owen is Assistant Director, but he serves as archivist and curator. Then there's the docents. We're on a very tight budget."

"Any relatives?"

"None. She was all alone in the world," she said with a tinge of sadness. "The Society was her family."

"Can you maybe just give me a little hint on what she was working on that was so important? "

"Mr. Owen would be very angry with me."

"You mean he tells everyone what to do and when to do it."

Moon's remark had its desired effect. "He most certainly

does not!" she shot back. "We volunteers work here without pay, to help the Society."

"Not to take orders from him," he added, fueling the fire.

"That's right."

"Now, what was Elaine Haskell working on again?"

"She was sorting out and referencing letters written by a soldier who served in the Civil War—a local boy named Stanford Short. There are hundreds of letters. They were sitting in a box in our attic for lord knows how long. Luckily, they were in a marvelous state of preservation. Elaine was ecstatic when she discovered them."

"Discovered them? Here?"

"Oh my, yes. Our attic is filled with artifacts. We don't know half of what's up there, because one can barely move around. You know, it wouldn't hurt for you to write about our space requirements."

"I might," he said, dangling a carrot to keep her talking. "Was there anything unique about the letters?"

"The boy was a marvelous writer. But then, so many people in those days were. Not like today, when a phone call or a fax will do. In many ways, they were better people than we, the people from that era. Not in so much of a hurry, so impatient with society. They had a sense of history then, Mr. Moon, and we've lost it. We are quick to judge our forebears by our standards, when we have no real understanding of them or their times. Elaine also felt that the tone of the letters and their points of origin might prove that Stanford Short read General Sherman's mail."

"Would that have been spectacular news?"

"Locally, it would have been exciting, but otherwise, no. Elaine was fascinated with the project, though. I hadn't seen her so involved in anything for a long time."

"Did she lose any of the letters? Were any of them missing?"

"No, not that I know of. I'm sure they're all here, in the archives. It's funny, though."

"What's funny?"

"The policeman who was here earlier also expressed a lot of interest in the Stanford Short letters. You know, he had on the oddest leather coat. It looked like an old duster, the kind we used to wear when going out for an automobile ride."

He could see her mind was beginning to wander, so he took her hand in his to say goodbye. It was cold, as though her heart couldn't spare the extra effort to pump blood to distant extremities.

"Goodbye Mister Moon," she said. "Have that elbow looked after."

He resisted the urge to kiss her on the cheek and call her mom.

As he walked back to the Rambler, Moon caught sight of a flash of red out of the corner of his eye, sure that he had seen Manny Edison disappear into the back yard of the adjacent home.

CHAPTER NINE

Y ou wouldn't find Moon's room at the Hotel Nelson featured in one of those snooty upscale home decorating magazines. Eighteen grand per year as editor and columnist at *The
Express* and child-support payments for three adolescent daughters had forced him into what he jokingly called "my luxurious accommodations." The room held an antique Murphy
bed which he'd refused to allow the management to remove
when they remodeled; a kitchenette in one corner; an old
mirrored dresser topped by a small TV and a VCR to play his
treasured classic movies; a frayed rag rug in the center of the
floor and a single straight-backed wooden chair.

The room's only window looked out over a wide park,
with majestic maples and a large, domed neoclassic library.
Just across the street was a tall marble column holding a statue
of Winged Victory, its base inscribed with the words: *In honor
of those who gave the greatest sacrifice in the War of the Great Rebellion,
1861-1865.*

As he stared at his reflection in the blotched mirror on
the wall next to his dresser, Moon was reminded of a photo
of Wild Bill Hickok he'd once seen in an encyclopedia. Heavy
bags—pale fleshy half-moons—accented gray eyes sunk into

a long, mournful face. Deep wrinkles creased the forehead, gray hairs peppered flowing rusty-blonde hair and drooping moustaches. He wasn't familiar with Hickok's personal history—but in his case, too much booze, brawling like a twenty year old, trying to live in the fast lane, was to blame for his pitiful appearance.

He dragged the chair to the window, cracked a cold beer from his two-foot-square refrigerator and stared at the Civil War monument, Winged Victory shrouded in snow.

Born and raised in Chicago in the Garfield Park neighborhood above his parents' corner saloon where they traded shots, beers and political barbs with the customers, Moon received a hard-nosed education at an early age.

His mother had been a machine Democrat. Toed the party line and busted her ass hustling votes. Her party loyalty was the reason the cops laid off the tavern, sending the bag men only at election time. Moon's memories of his mother were brief and disjointed. She died when he was ten—an old lady aged beyond her years by drink, chain-smoking and the long hours of tavern life.

As she lay in her coffin, surrounded by flowers and boozy customers, he knelt down and whispered the only prayer he knew; a brief appeal to God that he heard his friend Joey LaMacchia once recite. He couldn't remember exactly what it was, but it was something about Heaven and forgiveness. He didn't know any real prayers—for him church had been the saloon, with Ma and Pa dispensing political sermons and serving up communion boilermakers. He had leaned over and kissed his mother in her coffin. It put a chill on his lips that he could still feel after 33 years.

Born the night of the 1948 Truman-Dewey election, it was his Old Lady who had tagged Moon with the godawful name "Truman". Ma went into the hospital at noon, while the Old Man was out for Dewey, dragging winos to the polls.

He was positive they were finally going to put a Republican in the White House.

He was born at two in the morning, with Dad nowhere to be found. Harry Truman had won in a surprise upset, and when Dad struggled into the hospital at dawn, reeking of bourbon, with a half-dozen Have-A-Tampas poking from his shirt pocket he found Ma with a mile-wide grin, Moon in swaddling tucked in next to her, a copy of the 'Dewey Defeats Truman' issue of the Chicago Tribune spread out on the bed.

"Sydney," she'd said sarcastically, "meet your new son, Truman." She would relate the story many times over the years to her customers; her elbows on the bar, cackling.

Moon's Old Man never lived it down. He believed that Franklin Roosevelt and the Democratic Party were the cause of every problem in America, from World War Two to Chicago's cavernous pot holes. It was lucky that Ma was such a loyal Democrat. In a machine city like Chicago, his father's politics would have gotten the tavern boarded up. Moon's father was a half-assed businessman, but to his credit he was smart enough to put a lid on the Republican speeches after his wife died.

On his 70th birthday, his father collapsed behind the bar right after the Cubs had locked up the division title for the first time since 1945.

Moon was working in Southport by that time, and had become something of a celebrity as a fearless columnist for the Southport Times, but immediately drove down to Chicago to visit his father in the hospital when he got the news of his collapse. When Moon entered his darkened room he saw Pa flat on his back, a mass of sagging wrinkles with hollow cheekbones and eyes.

"Hi, son," his father said, smiling weakly. "Your sister just left."

"How's she doing, Pa?"

"Fine. Just fine. She says for you to come and see her in Joliet, whenever you get the chance."

"How are her kids and her husband?"

"Fine. I didn't see 'em, though. She come up by herself."

It was evident to Moon that Pa wouldn't leave the hospital, except in a box, but for some reason he was unable to cry.

"Lissen, sonny," his father had said. "I got a bet with Harvey MacCormack. My ten bucks against his twenny. I say the Cubbies'll take the play-offs. If I'm still in the hospital, you collect for me. You know Harvey. He'll welsh on a bet if you let him."

"Sure, Pa. I'll take care of it." His father had given him his last will and testament.

He died that night, before the Cubs dropped the play offs to the Padres, on a limp homer from the weak-hitting Steve Garvey and a muffed play by Leon "Bull" Durham.

At the funeral, Moon collared Harvey MacCormack and stuffed ten singles into his shirt pocket. "The old man wanted to make sure you got this, Harv," he said. "In case the Cubbies lost."

"Your pa was a good egg," said Harvey, wiping tears from his bloodshot eyes. He had a substantial toot on, bourbon heavy on his breath. "He never welshed on a bet." Harvey MacCormack had written his dad's epitaph, and Moon had it carved on the small square of marble that marked the family plot.

Two weeks after the funeral, Moon and his sister let the bank take the tavern and sold the few bits of furniture and old appliances left in the upstairs apartment. The few dollars they got from the sale paid for most of the Old Man's funeral. He gave his sister a dispassionate peck on the cheek and they went their separate ways: she to her salesman husband, three kids and ranch-style home in Joliet; Moon to his wife and three daughters and crumbling marriage in Southport. That had been seven years ago, and he hadn't seen her since. They had never been close as kids, either.

Moon got up from the chair and stared at himself in the mirror. "You were so proud of me, Pa," he said, "I wonder what you'd think of how I've screwed up my life."

And now he was going to screw his life up even more. Tomorrow he was going back to the Historical Society and ferret out the letters, and the hell with Manny Edison.

He sipped the last of the beer and hook-shot the empty can into the waste basket. It bounced out and rolled across the floor.

CHAPTER TEN

Tuesday, January 15, dawned bright and clear and not too cold, with a brilliant blue sky and high, puffy clouds. Smoke from factory chimneys froze in the winter sky—dirty gray against the bright blue. It was deadline day for Iraqi troops to retreat from Kuwait before attack by the U.S.-led coalition forces.

Tessie Allen's face appeared inside the beveled glass window of the Historical Society's front door. Moon wiggled the best little old lady wave he could manage. When that failed he again appealed to her motherly instincts by pointing to his elbow and mouthing some words.

She opened the door and poked her head into the frigid outside air. "We're not open today," she said, pointing at the hours painted on the glass.

Moon jammed a foot in the door and slid inside. "I just came to tell you my elbow is a lot better."

"That's nice. But I really must ask you to leave."

"Why are you afraid to talk to me? Is it that guy upstairs, Owen?" She glanced nervously behind her. "Are you afraid of him?"

"Mr. Owen feels that the circumstances surrounding Miss

Haskell's death are detrimental to the Society."

"I agree. But Haskell is dead, and we have to find out who did it."

"The police have a confession from the murderer. I read it in the newspaper last night."

"The man they have in custody is not the murderer."

"But the newspapers ...the police ..." Her tiny voice quavered and threatened to crack.

"Are wrong," Moon interrupted.

Tessie Allen was utterly confused, disoriented. "What do you want?" she pleaded.

"I'm interested in what kind of person Elaine Haskell was."

"She was a great lady."

"You told me that yesterday. If she was a great lady, she was a great lady with a hell-excuse my French-of a problem. I only met her once, and she was tanked."

"When did you meet her?" she shot back.

Good, thought Moon. She had her little old lady's dander up. She'd talk.

"The night she died. At a tavern."

"Was she drunk?"

"Very. Incoherent, almost."

She hung her head as if the shame was hers. "It was Elaine's continuing problem, you know. She could do almost anything but control her drinking. And now look where it's gotten her."

"Dead," Moon said. She winced. "What was she like from a professional standpoint?"

"She was the most intelligent woman I've ever met. She was a driven woman."

"Driven?"

"Oh, yes. Her father was owner of the *Southport Times*, before the Conrads bought it. Back in the nineteen forties. Actually it's more accurate to say that Charles Conrad senior *took* the paper from Daniel Haskell."

"I can believe that. From all I've heard, Conrad senior was a ruthless individual." (Like his prick kid, my ex-boss, thought Moon).

"Indeed. And Elaine always felt that her father had been cheated out of the paper. Research into the events surrounding her father's loss of the paper led her into the historical field."

"You said she was working on some Civil War letters before she died?"

"From Stanford Short. He served in the entire war, first in the Western theater, then in the East with Sherman's army."

"The march through Georgia?"

"Yes. His letters recount the horrors of the march quite poetically. Stanford Short was a marvelous writer."

"Can I see the letters?"

A shout from the mezzanine echoed through the home: "Elaine's research papers are not for public consumption!" A livid Owen was leaning over the second-floor railing. His feminine hands gripped the deeply polished mahogany rail tightly, his knuckles even whiter than his pasty complexion. Owen descended the staircase deliberately, heel to toe, step by step, like a chief of state ready for the band to strike up "Hail to the Chief." When he reached the bottom step, he jammed his fists into his hips, angry eyes fixed on a petrified Tessie Allen. It was supposed to be a show of masculine strength, but it more closely resembled a petulant child who hadn't gotten what he wanted.

"I believe you were asked to leave yesterday," he said to Moon. Tessie fiddled nervously with a string of bright, multicolored plastic beads circling her neck.

"I wasn't asked to leave, Owen," Moon replied. "I left of my own accord."

"Would you please leave again, then? Of your *own accord*,

of course."

Moon had to control his temper. "Thank you for your gracious assistance," he said to Tessie Allen. She nervously fingered the beads, like a rosary, looking at Owen all the while.

★★★

The snowplow crews were vacationing in the tropics, it seemed. Most of the streets were untouched, with large drifts blocking traffic.

Elaine Haskell's home was located in an area of substantial brick ranch homes, wide lawns and kids cavorting in the snow. In the front yard of the home adjacent to Haskell's, six kids were putting the finishing touches on a snowman. One ten-year-old boy was sticking twigs in the snowman for fingers. A girl the same age removed her bright red scarf and wrapped it around the snow man's neck. The boy laughed at the sight of the scarf and tossed a snowball at the girl. She screamed and tried to fire a snowball back, but the boy pushed her down and jumped on top of her, pinning her arms to the snow. She screamed "Joey!"—but there was no real fear in her voice.

Moon mused that he must have had some sort of relationship like that with girls when he was that age, but at forty-three, he couldn't remember them. He parked the car and walked up to the kids. As a father, Moon knew that kids could sometimes be a candid and important source of information. He started with a few no-brainers.

"Is the lady next door home?" he asked, pointing to Elaine Haskell's house. They rose from their adolescent embrace, encrusted with snow.

"No, mister," said the little girl. "She ain't home there no more. She's dead."

"Yeah, she's dead," echoed Joey.

The snow was wet and cold on Moon's feet. He wished

he'd worn boots. "Do you know how she died?" he asked the little girl. Her cheeks were flushed with the cold. He could see a few strands of blonde hair creeping out from under her parka hood. Her bright blue eyes matched the color of the winter sky. She made Moon think of his three daughters. Laura, his oldest, was about the same age.

"Somebody killed her, I think," Joey piped up. Hatless, his shock of black hair was speckled with snow. The boy had the spare look of the poet about him, even at his young age. He'd be trouble for the little girl in three or four years, thought Moon.

"When was she killed?"

"A coupla days ago, I think," said the little girl.

"At night," said the boy.

"Did you see anything?"

"Naw. We were sleeping. Everybody was sleeping. Even my mom and dad."

"You live around here?"

The boy pointed to the house on whose front lawn they were standing. The little girl pointed to the house on the other side. "I live there," she said. "And we didn't see nothing either. I told the other man the same thing."

"The other man?"

"He came before. He asked if anybody seen anything, too."

"What did he look like?"

"I don't know," said the girl. "He had a long red coat on. And a funny hat. He wasn't big, like you."

A woman poked her head out the front door of Joey's house. "Jo-wee! Come in for your clarinet lesson!"

"Aw, ma," protested Joey.

"Now!"

"Aw, shoot!" Joey said as he shuffled reluctantly toward the house, kicking at the snow.

The woman eyed Moon suspiciously. She was beefy as a

truck driver. "You want something, mister?"

"No," said Moon. "I was just admiring the snowman, that's all."

"Well, you've admired it. Now get off the lawn." She eyeballed Moon until he climbed into the Rambler and drove away. He'd come back after nightfall, when they'd be locked safely behind their doors. Out of sight, out of mind.

CHAPTER ELEVEN

Eight PM. Bombs were falling on Baghdad when Moon parked the Rambler three blocks from Elaine Haskell's house. Sirens and huge explosions echoed on his car radio. Well, they've gone ahead and done it, he thought. There was no turning back now. He remembered arguing with one of the pressmen at the *Times* about Saddam Hussein.

"We'll kick his butt in six days," the pressman had insisted.

"More like six months," Moon shouted back over the roar of the Goss Suburban presses. "The man's a cockroach ...a survivor. He'll go down in flames—if he goes down at all."

"Bet you a beer," he said as he wiped ink off his hands with a rag.

"I don't bet on war," Moon had said as he walked away.

The video war had locked everyone to their televisions, leaving the neighborhood deserted as Moon walked over the neatly shoveled sidewalk in front of little Joey's house. His shoes sank into the snow in front of Elaine Haskell's. He slogged around the side of her house to the back door. It was a thin aluminum screen door, with a hollow core door behind it. Not much to it. He was certain there would be no whistles or bells. Dead women set no burglar alarms. A quick shove at the lock with a screwdriver, a flick of the wrist, and it was open. He pulled a flashlight from his parka pocket.

He found himself standing in a lavish kitchen commanded by a large island with a six-burner stove set into a butcher-block top. Copper pots and pans hung from a rack bolted into the ceiling. A gourmet, thought Moon. He trained the beam on a wall, illuminating a large framed poster of an anorectic model sitting on the hood of a Rolls-Royce. "You can never be too rich or too thin," it said. He walked through the kitchen and into the living room, nearly falling over a large leather sofa that jumped out of the dark.

He sat on the sofa, scoping the room with the flashlight. There were two Chagall prints, a print of Picasso's "Blue Guitarist" as well as large photo reproductions of Civil War generals Lee and Grant. Some official-looking citations and awards. A large rolltop desk. Two hard-backed caned chairs. A thick, expensive-looking rug, with a geometric bright orange and blue pattern.

He examined Haskell's desk. The police had swept the place for prints and he could see evidence of their work in the disarray. They figured they had their man, and he figured anything they had left behind was fair game. He rolled the desk top up. The pigeon holes were filled with bills and receipts, paper clips and stamps. There were pens and pencils and a few loose papers on the desk. He riffled through them and found some office memos, personal notes, and a letter to a friend, congratulating her on the birth of her first child. There was also a typewritten note to the State Historical Society, requesting muster rolls and troop movements of the 33rd Wisconsin Infantry and the 1st Wisconsin Cavalry in the years 1861 - 1865. We're getting closer, thought Moon. A note, scribbled in pencil at the bottom, said: *Owen doubts authenticity of letters. Barber knows.*

Next to the letter was a small stack of typed sheets. Moon's heart leaped as he recognized what they must be: The Stanford Short letters, transcribed by Elaine Haskell. The first two sheets listed the letters in chronological order, from 1861 to 1865. The first letter was dated Chicago, March 28, 1861. He read by the flashlight beam.

Dear Mother:

A few spare moments I spend this morning in your service and acknowledge the very good letter you wrote me last week. It was quite a short one but then, you know I enjoyed it just as much and perhaps better.

"Matches, shoe bla-a-acking, shoe brushes?" says a little ragged boy at the door, having a good supply of both. Of course, we do not purchase. Great loads of flour barrels, hogsheads and hogs' heads, pigs's feet, hides, beef-skulls, eggs, ducks & meats of all descriptions—an everlasting lot of everything eatable and saveable pass the store every day—enough to furnish Southport people food for a month. I see a great many well-dressed people— but a great many here that look as though all they wore was begged. On Monday evening I called on Mary Pitkin—a sister of that Miss P., at Mrs. Dolittle's. Tuesday evening I went to a surprise party with the Scrantons & other friends-at Mrs. Dunham's. We had a nice time of course. Last evening I went to prayer-meeting at Clark St. and tonight I shall go to Mrs. Chase's to see about Aunt Libbie's dress. Am sorry the samples were not yet sent before but the delay was unavoidable. Have you a girl yet? If not, do get one immediately, and the money will come.

Did Pa receive a letter from me Tuesday? Should like to hear from it.

The temptations are many, but I trust with the principles of a true religion in my heart, and with the kind admonitions of dear parents I may be kept safe through all. Shall write to Freddie soon. When does examination come off?

Love to all the dear ones at home.

Your loving son,
Stannie

Moon's whisper echoed in the empty home. "What's so terrific about this?"

The next letter was dated April 21, 1861, again, from Chicago:

Dear Mother:

In the midst of all the excitement and business, my thoughts are brought to my home many times, especially on the Sabbath. Today is a most delightful and pleasant one to me while in my room, but while in the street my head runs wild almost with excitement and thoughts concerning the great question of the day. This week has been one continual scene of wild enthusiasm and military movements, Processions, Parading, Bon Fires, Meetings, etc. all the time. The principal streets of the city are thronged with men, women and children, Soldier Companies drilling, marching bands playing and everything but Sunday. But I suppose it cannot be avoided. Our two American principles of freedom and liberty must be preserved. Often when thinking about the great question of the day my heart jumps, sending a chill through my veins, inspiring my soul with courage to do anything in the cause of my country and liberty. I never had such feelings before. It seems as though I must do something to rescue my Native land from destruction and ruin though my efforts be ever so weak. The cause is a just one and I think any Christian can enter the soldier's life on our side of the question with the approbation of a Heavenly Father. I only hope that I am up to the task should I ever be called to battle.

All my love, dearest Mother and Father.

Stannie

The commitment, sense of purpose, and courage revealed

in the letter made Moon—a veteran of street marches of the
Sixties—uncomfortable. He read a third letter:

> Pittsburgh Landing, Tenn. April 10, 1862
> Dear Father:
> Though I wrote a short and disconnected note on the morning
> after the battle, that will relieve you of all anxiety, yet I must not
> fail to give an immediate answer to your two letters of Mar. 31
> and Apr. 3rd which also brought Jennie's and Grandmother's
> letters. They arrived last evening and being the first, after our hard
> fought battle, I assure you they were very, very acceptable. Two
> also came from Charlie which were, of course, very comforting.
> You certainly have heard of our recent engagement, yet may be in
> the dark as to who are the sufferers. I hope my note may have
> speedy passage and relieve our Southport friends of the anxiety
> they surely must have. You will probably hear that our battery is
> lost and "cut to pieces" yet all such reports are false. We lost no
> guns, while but one of us was killed and five wounded. We were on
> the field 9 hours Sunday, but kept in reserve the day following,
> though we were moving forward into position Monday afternoon
> when the rebels commenced their flight. I cannot describe the fury
> of the engagement during the two days—and very much doubt the
> ability of anyone to do so. To say that it was terrible would be a
> very tame description of the bloody conflict. The only true idea of
> this horrible fight could be gained by a sight of the field on which
> we fought for two days...
> Dead and wounded soldiers by the hundreds, Federal and Rebel
> side by side, hundreds of dead horses, disabled guns, caissons,
> harness and all kinds of arms, clothings, blankets, camp equipage,
> baggage wagons, and demolished camps, in wild confusion. The
> horrible sights we were obliged to behold on every side were enough
> to chill the blood of the most vile murderer. Fredericktown,
> Belmont and Donelson cannot be compared with it. God grant that
> we may never be called to see the likeness of it again. The attack

on our position was entirely unexpected and consequently the rebels were on us almost before we knew that they were within a dozen miles. The attacking force Sunday is supposed to have been about 90,000.

They drove us inch by inch through our own camps, about two miles, when night stopped the deadly work. With a reinforcement of a portion of Buel's army we attacked the enemy at daylight on Monday morning. (They had also been reinforced during the night by some 15 or 20,000). We drove the rebels back over the same ground we had lost the day before, and about three o'clock they commenced retreating and in an hour the battle was ended.

I despair of giving you any better or more definite idea of the fight. Should I ever get home, I then can give you the particulars. As it is the largest battle of the war, much attention will doubtless be given to the writing of a full description which you certainly will see and then perhaps know something of our last struggle and I sincerely hope our final one.

What can I say of God's goodness to me? Words cannot express the gratitude and thankfulness I have in my heart to Him who has kindly preserved my life through another conflict.

Affectionately,
Your Stannie

There was a note scribbled in the margin of this letter: Shiloh, April, 1862. He assumed it was Elaine Haskell's handwriting.

"Jesus," he thought, imagining the fury of the battle. "I don't think I would've made it through a fight like that. I'd have bolted and run." He carefully folded the copies and the handwritten note and put them into his pocket. No one would ever know they were missing.

As he made his way back through the kitchen, he heard a secretive rattling. He killed the flashlight and held his breath.

Sweat crept up his collar. Someone was fiddling with the back door, trying to get in.

He took a chance. "Who is it?" he demanded in an authoritative voice. Teenage experience as an apprentice cat burglar with a gang of Chicago Irish kids—most of whom had ended up in the slammer—had taught Moon that a loud mouth could scare away a thief as easily as a Saturday-night special. The rattling stopped, and then he heard footsteps crunching in the snow, receding into the darkness.

"Probably some kid," he reassured himself, "trying for an easy score by knocking off the dead lady's home."

He slipped out the door onto the back porch. An orange flash streaked out of the dark from between two snow-covered evergreens. He heard the pop! and whine of the shot as it screamed past his face. Then he heard the crunch of jogging feet and ran toward the sound, following the gunman's footprints in the snow. He should have run in the opposite direction, but he was pissed off and wanted to throttle whoever it was who had shot at him.

Moon raced past the evergreens, leaped over a four-foot chainlink fence, knocked over a couple of garbage cans in the neighbor's yard and then tore down their driveway and out into the center of the next street, where he lost the footprints and sounds of the gunman. He bent over, hands on his knees, breathing in stressful fits and starts.

"I'm in no shape for this shit," Moon groaned as he slowly made his way back to his car.

CHAPTER TWELVE

1865

Short was feeling relaxed for the first time since the armistice. He had gotten the General's letter off to his father and had Meriwether Pickens put in the guard house. With some free time on his hands, he strolled out of the front yard of the mansion, down the path leading to the soldiers' camp. Charlie Fay and the First Wisconsin had ridden in from Jones' Cross Roads the night before. He wanted to talk to some of the Wisconsin boys. They were all old friends, especially Charlie Fay, whom Short hadn't seen in over a year, since Sherman had obtained Short's transfer to his headquarters.

The war years had been hard, and the past year had been the worst. After the horrendous battles for Atlanta, the march through Georgia and up the Carolinas had been a cakewalk, as the Confederacy had concentrated the last of its once-formidable forces with Lee in the siege at Petersburg and with John Bell Hood's vicious attacks on Nashville and Franklin in the east.

Sherman had marched virtually unopposed through the heart of the Confederacy, tearing up railroad track, burning homes, farms and factories, laying waste to once fertile farmland that would not recover from the devastation for years.

It was this that had troubled Short most: watching the civilians, especially the women and children, endure such terrible hardships. Riding alongside Sherman one day they had come upon a smoldering farm—from the looks of it once a prosperous estate. They had ridden by the ruins stoically, the General staring straight ahead while he bit down on his cigar. His favorite mount, Sam, pushed the rest of the small troop at its usual murderous pace.

They passed by a row of small, drafty slave cabins that had been spared the torch. There were no slaves about, but two white women stood outside one of the cabins, their elegant hoop skirts now tattered and dirty. One of them ran up to the General, her hoop skirt flying up and down, revealing filthy petticoats underneath. She stood at the side of the road and shook her fist at them as they passed.

"Yankee soldiers!" she howled, hate etched on her face. "You murdered my baby! She died last night, cold and starving! You murdered my baby!"

General Sherman pulled the raw-boned Sam to a halt and stared down at the woman, his face like stone. "Madam," he said icily. "I am truly sorry for you and your child. But it is not we who have murdered your baby. It is you who are the murderer. You and the whole of the Confederacy, who, by waging war on the lawful government of the United States, have brought this terrible hardship upon yourselves. Stop waging war, and the deaths will stop. It is as simple as that." He kicked his heels lightly into Sam's flanks, and the troop moved on, leaving the woman on her knees in the roadside, convulsively sobbing.

"Stannie," Sherman said. "I don't want to appear a hard man, but what I said back there is true. If it weren't for these damnable Southern females, who have shamed their men to continue the fight, this war would have ended last year. I am truly sorry for that woman and her child. But until these rebels cease their unlawful pursuit of secession from the legal government of the United States, more children will die." The General spurred Sam on, leaving his small escort in a cloud of dust.

One-armed General Oliver O. Howard, thick beard powdered with dust, muttered under his breath. "He's missed the point, as always. This is God's war, a war to free the slaves and restore the rights of man, and planned by the lord God almighty."

Short pushed his mount faster, to get ahead of Howard. He did not want to be trapped into hearing one of the pompous, pious General's overbearing sermons.

Now it was all over. It had been two days since Joe Johnston had surrendered to Sherman. Short had seen many of Johnston's soldiers wandering the road, heading south: shoeless, hatless, in tattered uniforms and looking as if they hadn't eaten in weeks. Seeing them this way, Short had begun to respect them for the first time. For so many years he had hated the South, its armies and all they stood for. But now, seeing the defeated soldiers up close, he saw in their misery and despair that they were flesh and blood, like him and they wanted to go home. They had tucked a few meals of federal rations into their bellies and plodded on. Under these circumstances he would have done the same thing, Short thought. He wondered what it would have been like, if these soldiers had been the victors. He tried to imagine them sweeping through Chicago and up the lake shore to Southport, but he couldn't. It was unimaginable.

As Short neared the camp he could hear filtering through the trees the clanking of tin cups, the strumming of a banjo, and a group of soldiers singing "Lorena." As he quickened his pace, he could hear Charlie Fay's voice above the din. Charlie Fay had been his best friend back home and they had enlisted on the same day and seen action in the same battles.

Fay would probably marry Short's sister, Elaine, one day.

Short broke into a trot. "Fay!" he yelled, "Charlie Fay! Where are you?"

"I'm over here, you horse's ass!" shouted Fay.

Short saw the tall, lanky Fay standing over a smoldering campfire, pouring himself a cup of coffee. Fay smiled broadly at him, and with that smile Short knew the war was really over. He had made it through four years and soon, he'd be home. It was all right. Everything was all right. They wrapped their arms around each other, hugged and wept.

"It's over, Charlie," muttered Short as tears ran down his cheeks. He didn't see Meriwether Pickens, skulking behind a tree a few yards away.

CHAPTER THIRTEEN
1991

The new war escalated during the night. Iraqi missiles had hit Tel Aviv. The world held its breath, wondering if the Israelis would counterattack. Closer to home, a short news item on page thirteen of the *Chicago Tribune* described a peace march in Southport that had been a flop, with only a hundred people showing up. In Chicago, more than 2,000 had marched down State Street, but still a feeble effort compared to some of the marches Moon had participated in against the Viet Nam War. In 1970, he'd marched with 50,000 others—the air charged with electric anticipation, incense, and clouds of marijuana fumes. It had seemed to everyone at the time that they were participating in a new American Revolution. But that was in the days before the reign of Rolex watches, BMWs, Perrier, and leveraged buy-outs. The "Revolution" had succumbed to the good life, he mused. Who wanted to worry about the state of the world when a new Italian trattoria had just opened up down the street?

Sam, the proprietor of the coffee shop and lunch counter in the Hotel Nelson, knelt on one knee behind his counter and fired up a cigarette. "I shoulda been a baker," he said. "Yeah, I shoulda been a baker."

Sam took a long drag off his coffin nail. "I get up at five a.m. anyway. I coulda been working alone, at the oven, not fryin' eggs for weirdos." He nodded in the direction of a man at the counter with two day's growth of stubble, hollow eyes and a head of wild white hair. He was conversing in sotto voce with the two sunny side up eggs on his breakfast plate. They glared mutely back at him like bright yellow eyes.

"Mr. Venskunis was the baker in our neighborhood," said Moon. "His bakery was just down the block from Pa's tavern. Ma used to send me down there with a buck every Sunday morning, and I'd get two loaves of hot bread. I'd always tear a a piece off one loaf and eat it on the way home, and Ma would always whack me in the head for doing it."

Sam stared at his grease-specked ceiling. "Yup, a baker's what I shoulda been."

"Mr. Venskunis always looked dog-tired, Sam. Baking bread is a hard life."

"Nothin' could be worse than this, Moon. The hotel's clientele is gettin' worse. More guys like that one." He jerked his head toward the whispering man. "Lot of these people comin' in now. Government pays for 'em. They should be in the loony bin, not out on the streets." The man was now holding a heated argument with the eggs, and Moon half-expected the eggs to stand and shout back.

Manny Edison slid onto the stool next to Moon. A short black man with a large Afro like a black dandelion gone to seed shot a sidelong glance at the cop and slunk guiltily out of the room.

"Coffee, Sam," said the cop.

Moon motioned to Edison's Mets cap, balanced atop his greasy locks. "I hate the Mets," he said.

"Oh, yeah. Cubs fan, aren't you?" Manny Edison reached into his shirt pocket and pulled out a buck for coffee, flashing the butt end of his pistol tucked in its shoulder holster.

"Who do you think you are, Pancho Villa?"

"No spics, Mr. Newspaper Writer. Don't compare me with no spics."

"Sorry. I wouldn't want them to feel insulted. Someone took a shot at me last night. Wouldn't have been you, would it?"

"Maybe somebody was tryin' to pop you for a payback on one of your columns. But not me. If I shoot at somebody, he goes down. For good."

Moon tried to read his eyes to see if he was lying. They were like twin sludge pools: slicked over, masking polluted horrors beneath. Edison tapped the side of his nose.

"I know, Manny. Your nose. The famous talking proboscis."

"It's been telling me things, Mr. Writer."

"Like what?"

"Like maybe you been messing around in business that don't concern you. It also tells me that maybe you got a lead on something that could be very valuable."

"Now what could that be?"

"Maybe those missing letters, huh?"

"I take it you mean the Stanford Short letters. Why are they so important?"

"Maybe they got the Haskell woman killed."

"What about the innocent man you've got locked up for the murder? What's he say about that?"

"Not much. He hung himself in his cell last night."

Moon sucked in air through gritted teeth.

"Don't tell me you're surprised," said Edison. "The guy was a walkin' time bomb."

"How could it happen? Where were your jailers? "

"Hey, what are you getting all worked up about? It's no problem of yours."

Moon fought the urge to grab Edison's buzzard neck and throttle him. "No problem of anybody's, is it, Manny? He was just a nobody anyway."

"Guy wants to commit suicide, ain't nothing nobody can do about it. I think ..."

Moon cut him off. "You think? Or does your nose think, snot-for-brains?" Sam edged away as Manny reached inside his coat and fingered the walnut handle of his .44.

"Bringing your partner in on this too, I see." Moon nodded at Edison's hand on the pistol. "You, your nose and your forty-four."

"So tell me, Mr. Smart Guy Writer. What about those letters?"

They were eye to eye. "If I did know—which I don't," Moon said deliberately, "I sure as hell wouldn't tell some scumbag rip-off cop like you, now would I?"

The pistol appeared as if by magic, cold steel barrel pressed against Moon's cheek. Edison pulled the hammer back slowly, cocking it with a threatening click.

Moon stared over the pistol into Edison's rheumy eyes. "Go ahead and do it. And if you think I ripped your tits in those last columns, you haven't seen anything yet."

"How you gonna write a column if you're dead, Mr. Writer?" His expressionless face was as cold as the steel of his pistol.

"I'll come back from the dead and coach Sam. He'll write it for me."

Manny Edison smiled and grunted and then shoved the pistol back into his shoulder holster.

"You got balls, Moon. I'll give you that much. You sure as hell got balls." He sauntered cockily out of the restaurant.

"See?" Moon said with false bravado to Sam, who was cringing behind the counter. "The pen is mightier than the sword."

Sam nervously fired up a second cigarette, oblivious to the first cigarette balanced on the edge of the counter. "Jesus," he said, "Fuckin' with Manny Edison. You're nuts."

Moon's hands trembled at the outrageous foolishness of what he'd done. He gulped the last of his coffee and tossed a buck on the counter. Sam shakily blew smoke from his cigarette ceilingward, like a genie released from a bottle.

CHAPTER FOURTEEN

Tessie Allen looked absolutely beside herself when she saw Moon in the front parlor, signing the guest registry. It was an open day for the Museum and he didn't have to freeze outside, trying to worm his way in.

He stomped snow off his shoes and smiled. "How's it going, Miss Allen?"

"Why do you keep pestering me?" she whispered.

"Just lending my support to the Society," he whispered back as he dropped a five-dollar bill into a clear acrylic box labeled DONATIONS, where it nestled next to a solitary single and two shiny quarters. "Aren't you going to show me around?"

"Wait," she whispered again. "I'll get one of the other docents."

"I'd prefer your company." He touched her arm lightly. "Why are we whispering?"

"I don't know," she said with irritation and a little too loudly. A wrinkled female head with a shock of white hair and two round brown eyes peeked around a door jamb, surprise etched on her face.

"Hush, Hazel!" said Tessie Allen, annoyed. The head jerked

back quickly at the reprimand. "They're all so nosy."

"Who?"

"The docents—a bunch of white-haired old ladies who sit in the back room, drinking coffee, eating cookies and gossiping. We don't get many visitors here. Sometimes we have more docents sitting in the back room than we have visitors." Moon chuckled at her reference to old ladies.

"Now, what do you want?" she asked.

"I'm interested in your Civil War artifacts."

"Not the letters. I've had enough trouble over them already."

"No, of course not. I'd just like to see whatever else you have."

"We have a Civil War room upstairs, if you'll follow me." She climbed the stairs aggressively, surprising for someone of her size and age. Moon was hard-pressed to keep up with her. His most vigorous exercise was drinking beer and shooting pool, so he was panting when they reached the second floor.

Tessie led him into a room with a huge blue battle flag on one wall, cracked with age, peppered with ancient bullet holes. He could still read its inscription: "Southport Volunteers For Union & Liberty." On the walls were a brace of pistols, two crossed muskets, posters calling for volunteers, and a large array of Civil War photographs, most of them featuring proud young men posed with sabers or rifles, ready to march off to do battle with the rebels in the name of liberty. Moon thought of Stanford Short's letters, his commitment to the Union cause, and he wondered how many of the boys in the photos had died in defense of their ideals.

"It's almost like a shrine, isn't it?" said Tessie in a hushed, reverent voice.

"Impressive." A photo on the wall beckoned Moon. A dozen resolute young Union men stared out from the tintype. Underneath was the typeset caption: "Co. I, 1st Wis.

Cavalry, which participated in the March through Georgia and the capture of Confederate President Jefferson Davis."

"Which one of these boys is Stanford Short?"

Tessie stiffened and clasped her hands tightly to her stomach.

Moon pressed her. "Didn't he serve in this unit?"

"He did. But you said you weren't here for the letters."

"I'm not. I am interested in Stanford Short, however. There's nothing in the rules that says I can't ask questions about him, is there?"

"This is he." Tessie reached around Moon and pointed to a young man in the center of the photograph, soldier's cap at a cocky angle on his head.

Moon thought he could see a rosy-cheeked flush in the cherubic face. "He can't be more than twenty-one," he said.

"Actually, he's twenty in this photo," replied Tessie. "But that wasn't so young for soldiers in that war. Some as young as ten served, and saw battle."

Moon decided to take a chance. "I'm convinced Short's letters have something to do with Elaine Haskell's murder."

Her face displayed polite surprise. "How can they? They have no importance, outside of their local historical value. Thousands of young men wrote letters home during the war."

"But these letters are special, aren't they?"

"They're more informative and better written than most, but that's not enough to murder for. And I can't think of anyone who would want to kill poor Elaine—for those letters or for any other reason. There must be some sort of curse on the letters."

"What do you mean, 'curse'?"

"Because of what happened to Stanford Short."

Moon raised his eyebrows. "What happened?"

"It was very tragic. He was killed on April twenty-ninth, eighteen sixty-five. The war was all but over, when a sniper from a renegade Confederate battalion shot him. We have his obituary. I can make a copy for you." She left Moon staring again at the photo of Stanford Short, and she returned moments later with a photocopy and handed it to him.

Moon put the paper in his pocket. "Thank you. I'll read it later. Now, will you tell me about the letters?"

Tessie Allen relented. "Oh, why not. What would you like to know?"

"Where did Elaine Haskell find them?"

She nodded upward. "In the attic, like I told you before. We have thousands of artifacts up there. They were wedged between some books on a shelf."

"Can I see the attic?"

Tessie paused and thought a moment before she spoke. "It's not open to the public."

"You said it'd be good if the columnist for *The Express* got up there and saw the magnitude of your storage problem, didn't you? We may be able to free some more money out of the city for an addition to the museum."

Tessie grimaced, but then she yielded and led him up a narrow stairway to the third floor, which had once been the mansion's grand ballroom, but now housed an amazing clutter of paintings, trunks, boxes, papers, knick-knacks stacked haphazardly, making it nearly impossible to squeeze through.

Moon struggled to move between cases of old musical instruments —dented tubas, horns, banjos—and a long table-top covered with walking sticks—ranging from elegant, gold-tipped and custom-made to old pieces of driftwood, intricately carved—each a reflection of its long-dead owner's personality. There were 19th-century wedding gowns with yellowed and dusty lace, and hundreds of daguerreotypes and tintypes of unnamed people. Altogether tens of thousands of artifacts were boxed, bagged, bundled and tied—memories of a Southport frozen in time.

"Where were the letters found?" Moon asked her as he brushed dust off his shoulder and stared at the portrait of a wide-eyed, raven-haired woman in a 1930s evening dress, painted by an obviously untalented artist.

"Here," she gestured, pointing to a row of metal shelves. Moon wedged between them, maneuvering to where she stood.

"They were here, on the shelves." She reverently fingered the narrow slot where the letters had rested. "They must have come in with the rest of the Short family endowment, but somehow they were misplaced. They sat here for years."

"How many years?"

She touched an ancient finger to her lower lip. "Oh, let's see ...we got the endowment around the turn of the century. I know it was before the Great War, so it had to have been at least ninety years ago."

"And the letters sat here all that time?"

"Yes. It's not unusual for that to happen. I would imagine that many historical societies around the country are sitting on valuable material they know nothing about. They often lack the funds to hire people to catalog their collections. We have a particularly acute problem here in Southport. You will mention it in your column?"

"I will." The newsman's credo, thought Moon: Promise anything, cut any throat, to get the story. He followed her through the musty clutter, down the steps and back into the Civil War room.

"Can I read the rest of the letters?"

"No. Mr. Owen would be furious!"

"Let me ask you a question, Miss Allen. Why do you allow Owen to dress you down the way he does?"

"I'm an old woman, Mr. Moon. You're too young to understand what I'm saying, although you've reached middle age and let me add that you're not aging well. I'm eighty years old and I've seen a lot. The years have softened me to people like Mr. Owen. In spite of his age, he's nothing more than a little boy—a frightened, misunderstood little boy, at that."

As if on cue, Mr. Owen strutted into the room. "Miss Allen, someone has been going through Stanford Short's letters. Was it you?"

"No, it wasn't me." Moon could see that lying pained her.

"The letters were out of sequence when I opened the box just now. Someone has obviously gone through them."

"It wasn't me," she said again, with a little less conviction.

"It will be impossible—do you hear me, *impossible*—to continue Elaine's work if those letters are tampered with." Tessie Allen looked as if she was about to break down and cry. Little boy or no, Moon had had his fill of him.

"Put a sock in it, shrimp," Moon said in his best tough-guy voice.

Outraged, Owen's face grew beet-red behind his oversize glasses.

"Last night," Moon said. "An innocent man hanged himself in his jail cell because of those letters, so you better let me take a look at them before the cops wise up and seize them as evidence. You may never get them back."

"That's unlikely," said the scholar, contemptuously brushing off Moon's weak bluff. "The police have terminated Elaine's case." He turned his attention to Tessie Allen. "Miss Allen," he ordered. "May I see you in my office?"

She followed him out of the room, looking worriedly back at Moon as Owen led the way.

Moon walked slowly back to the photo of Stanford Short. "What is it you did, old buddy, that has caused all this death so many years later?"

The boy's face stared back mutely, frozen by a camera snapped 130 years before.

CHAPTER FIFTEEN

1865

I︎t had taken ten dollars for the corporal to turn loose Meriwether Pickens once they were out of sight of Stanford Short. Mr. High and Mighty, thought Pickens as he headed into the woods. He would have to lay low for a few days. Short might be a sniveling little skunk, but he was still a captain and this was still the army and he could cause untold trouble for him.

Pickens hung around in the woods and the fringe of the soldiers' encampment for most of the day, trying to figure out how he was going to get Sherman's letter out of the Captain's possession. He was going to have to steal it from Short's room, and for that to happen, Short would have to be gotten out of the way somehow.

Meriwether Pickens was a cunning man, the worst of a bad lot. His father, who was often away from home for weeks at a time, left his huge brood to fend for themselves. His mother had died giving birth to her seventeenth child, and Meriwether, the oldest, had taught his siblings the fine arts of picking pockets and bullying neighborhood children into giving them their pennies and school lunches. When the war began, Meriwether saw the opportunity to get out of the house and get paid for it to boot.

The old man, nearly toothless from rot, had snatched the first pay scrip out of Merriwether's hand. "Gimme that!" he commanded, and Pickens had meekly aquiesced, frightened as always of his father's violcnt and uupredictable nature. He followed his pa down to Rennick's Tavern and watched him lose it all in an all-night poker game with a group of squinty-eyed professional card sharps that picked him apart like turkey buzzards.

Pickens' conflict with Short had started early. He had mustered in with men from all over Wisconsin at Camp Henry, adjacent to Southport's city cemetery and had trained all winter. Men like Short, who had enlisted even before the rebels shelled Fort Sumter, managed the regiment and whipped the men into shape. "Pick up your feet, Pickens!" Short commanded during training exercises. "Clean your tent, Pickens! Fall out, Pickens!"

Pickens had taken to calling Short "Mr. High and Mighty," behind his back, and did his best to shirk his responsibilities. But he remained cautious of Short. Although not wealthy themselves, Short's parents were professors, and tutored many of the children of Southport's wealthy elite, which enabled the Shorts to exert a profound influence on them.

Life at Camp Henry had been wretched for Pickens. He was constantly on punishment detail, made to do the most menial tasks, and Short had even recommended that he be mustered out of the regiment. But wretched as his life was, Pickens eventually realized it beat the hell out of home and he shaped up enough to keep himself in the army. The food was good, and there were no mobs of howling kids to pester him at all hours of the day and night, or drunken father to commandeer his pay. The worst of it had been the winter, when many men had died in their tents for want of warm bedding. The women of Southport responded by knitting woolen socks, blankets and mittens for the freezing men.

When the regiment moved out of camp to head south to war they had paraded through the city, led by their colonel on his magnificent stallion: 1,150 men bound for glory. The citizens of Southport had lined the streets and cheered them on.

But all the training and all the cheering had been nonsense to Pickens and the other men until they reached an unknown place called Shiloh, Tennessee. When the first screaming rebels rushed the Federal encampments, catching the sleeping Union army by surprise, pandemonium broke loose. Pickens had grabbed his gun and jumped out of his tent with the rest of them, but when he saw the men around him dying like flies, he disappeared into the trees and hid there for most of the morning, until the Union army had regrouped and mounted a counterattack. A lieutenant on horseback had spotted Pickens skulking in the woods, pulled out his saber and threatened, "Get up man, and get into the fight or I'll cut you in two myself!" Pickens begrudgingly moved into battle. Men were shrieking, howling; the whizzing bullets were so thick that they cut the trunks of trees in half. Pickens stuck close to the lieutenant with the saber, and when the fighting got so confused that it was impossible to tell Union from Confederate, he fired his one and only shot of the battle of Shiloh, hitting the lieutenant squarely in the center of his back, knocking him off his horse and killing him instantly. "That's for you, you bastard," he smirked. For the rest of the fight he kept well to the rear, always trying to look like he was endeavoring to get into the battle, in case another officer took notice of him.

After Shiloh, Pickens wheedled his way into the position of a camp steward. "No more fighting for me," he reasoned. "Let the others get killed or have their legs and arms shot away." He began to drink again, and for that he had been paraded around the camp grounds—stripped naked and wearing a barrel with "Drunkard" painted on the side. He got even with the man who turned him in. One overcast night when the full moon was buried behind the clouds, Pickens waited for him behind a wagon and when the sergeant strolled by, he sneaked up behind him and hit him on the head with a cast iron frying pan. "Sumbitch!" Pickens had cursed as the terrible blow split the sergeant's skull, splattering brains on his shirt. The sergeant had miraculously lived, and though it couldn't be proven, Pickens was widely suspected as the attacker. He never denied the charge, and other men began to give him a wide berth.

Now Pickens had the chance to lay his hands on some real money and Short had confused the issue. Pickens had sneaked into Sherman's room while the general was away, looking for something to steal, and had spotted the unfinished letter on the table. As he struggled to mouth the words, he heard the general returning and was forced to jump into a closet and hide. From the hideaway, Pickens watched the general put the finishing touches on the letter, Short's arrival and conversation with Sherman, and the subsequent puzzling drama of the false letter and spilled coffee.

When Short had pocketed the real letter, Pickens assumed that Short's motives were the same as his: personal aggrandizement and greed. He couldn't conceive of another motive for the theft. But now Short had the letter, and Pickens wanted it.

Then he had seen Short strolling down the dusty road toward camp—whistling, no less—and Pickens followed carefully behind, keeping to the cover of the woods, pondering how he was going to get into Short's room without the captain's knowledge.

CHAPTER SIXTEEN

1991

"Moon, I'm so sorry."

"Not as sorry as Mark Kieth, Sally. He never should have been put in jail. Maybe if I had just gotten to those Stanford Short letters, none of this would have happened."

"Don't blame yourself. Did you ever consider that those missing letters may have had nothing to do with Elaine Haskell's death?"

"Never. Especially since Manny's shown so much interest in them. He's a man with a mission, Detective Edison. That mission is dirty money, and those letters stink to high heaven with it."

"I don't agree."

"Haskell was murdered for a reason—a well-thought out reason—which discounts Mark Keith's confession."

"If the letters are the cause of her murder, why haven't the police pursued that angle?"

"Hell, Sally. They spend ninety-five percent of their time and the taxpayers' money chasing down one percent of the population—the same offenders, over and over. They get a major case like this one and a quick confession, they're going to sit on it and savor the applause. You really can't expect them to do anything else."

"But who would murder for old letters?"

"Maybe someone who would want to publish them. I've known writers who would do more for less. There are thousands of people out there determined to write the great American novel. Do you know how hard it is to get published these days? Damn near impossible. A find like the Stanford Short letters could launch the right person on a fantastic career. He could write his own ticket. Why else would somebody shoot at me?"

"Who shot at you? When?"

Moon told her about the gunman in the bushes at Elaine Haskell's house.

She furrowed her brows and pursed her lips, angry and concerned. "Moon, you'd better leave this alone. Now."

"I can't let a man take the rap for a crime he didn't commit."

"Then again, maybe Mark Keith *was* guilty. Maybe he hit Elaine out of frustration, or maybe he was going to rob her, and then he panicked."

"I'm not going to make that assumption until I've followed every lead to its logical conclusion."

"I really think I just gave you the logical conclusion. Moon ..." She was cut off by her ringing telephone. She walked over to it and picked it up. "Hello? Yes. Yes, he's here. Well, we were just going to eat dinner. All right. Just a minute." She covered the mouthpiece with her hand. "It's a Tessie Allen. She wants to talk to you. Take the phone in my bedroom if you want some privacy."

Moon went into her bedroom and picked up the phone. "Hello, Miss Allen?"

"Mr. Moon?" said Miss Allen. "I'm sorry to interrupt your dinner. They told me at your hotel that you might be at this number."

Moon made a mental note to kick Sam's fanny for giving out Sally's number to a stranger. "I wasn't hungry anyway," he replied. "I'm still shook up about Mark Keith's suicide, the man they were holding for Elaine Haskell's murder." He heard Sally listening in on the other phone. Some privacy, he thought.

Tessie's distress was evident over the wire. "If I had only voiced my suspicions sooner. I feel responsible for that poor man."

"What suspicions? Was it about the letters?"

"I'm at the Society. In the archives. I'd like you to come down here. Right now."

"Can't it wait?"

"No. I'm afraid something will happen to them."

"Them?"

"The other letters from Stanford Short. I've got them here for you."

Moon couldn't hide the excitement in his voice. "I'll be right over."

"There's something more than just the letters. I want you to see it. It may be what you're looking for."

"Keep the letters where you found them until I get there. Open the back door for me and wait in the archives."

"All right, but hurry. That poor man. That poor, poor man."

As Moon hung up the phone, Sally walked into the bedroom.

"Did you hear it, Moon?"

"Hear what?"

"The other click on the line. Somebody else was listening in on her end. He hung up before I did."

CHAPTER SEVENTEEN

Eerily silhouetted by the winter night, the Historical Society reminded Moon of the mansion on the hill behind the Bates' Motel in *Psycho*. He pulled the Rambler up to the curb, hopped out and walked to the rear of the mansion. As he had requested, Tessie Allen had left the door open. Moon was unfamiliar with the layout of the building from the back, and he cursed himself for not bringing along a flashlight. He grabbed a handrail and slowly climbed the back steps, fumbling for a light switch he didn't find. Somehow he made it to the second floor without mishap. He felt his way through a darkened office area and another hallway before he found the archives. He could see a dim light at the back of the room, near the end of the stacks.

"Tessie?" he called tentatively as he moved toward the light. He heard no reply. He turned a corner and looked down the aisles between the long shelves. Between the sixth and seventh stacks, he saw her tiny body stretched out on the floor—a baby bird fallen from its nest, eyes closed as if asleep. A small reading light clamped to one of the bookshelves cast soft shadows over her corpse. Tessie's dress, one she might have worn to church, was hiked up over her knees. The tiny flowers on the dress and the dim light almost made her look young again. He resisted the urge to pull the hem down and cover her legs. Death should be a dignified, private affair, thought Moon, staring down at the corpse. He felt like a reluctant peeping tom and turned his head in embarrassment for her, and as he did, he heard running feet somewhere behind him. He moved instinctively toward the sound.

As he inched down the hallway that ran the length of the second floor, he encountered a series of rooms outfitted in period style, each representing a Southport business of the past century. Moon began to probe them in the dark.

Moonlight streaming through a small window in the first room enabled him to see that it was a reconstructed turn-of-the-century barbershop. A red-and-white striped pole, a barber's chair with a store-window dummy dressed in Gay Nineties style seated in it, and a barber behind, trimming his customer's hair. The room was empty.

He moved on to another room, which housed a replica of an old-fashioned ice cream shop. A large sign reading "Southport Sweet Shop" was hung over a counter topped with glass jars filled with brightly-colored hard candies. There were four soda fountain chairs at the counter and another sign reading "Please Do Not Lean On The Glass." Like the barbershop, the moonlit room was empty.

He cautiously searched four more rooms: a dentist's office, a newspaper printer, a general store and a room with a turn of the century telephone switchboard. As Moon moved between the rooms and the hallway, he had the unsettling feeling that he was a needle stitching twin threads of past and present in his search for Tessie Allen's killer.

Each room was empty, save their artifacts and the musty smell of the past. "I know you're in here, you bastard!" he shouted. "You like to kill old ladies, huh? How about trying me out for size?" As he stood clenching his fists, he heard running feet, racing through the first floor.

He shot down the stairs. The feet were again below him, now running through the basement. He followed the sound to a set of concrete steps, found a light switch on the wall at the bottom of the stairs and hit it, suddenly illuminating a large hall filled with old farm machinery: mowers, reapers, wagons and plows—sharp metal angles and edges throwing hawk-like shadows on the wall. He winced as a row of rusted, yet lethal-looking teeth, of a large ancient mower menacingly brushed his pants cuff.

At the far end of the basement was a smaller room housing a replica of a blacksmith's shop. Horseshoes, horse collars, a giant bellows, hammers, three large leather aprons on the wall, and an anvil that looked like it weighed a ton.

A battered wooden counter cut the room in half, and from behind it Moon heard the sound of heavy breathing—someone who had stopped and crouched to catch his breath, like an exhausted rat racing on a wheel.

Moon inched up to the counter, put both hands on its rough-hewn surface, and slowly leaned over to look behind it, when he heard a sound behind him and tried to turn to meet it. What felt like an anvil hit him a glancing blow on the head. At the same moment a high-pitched voice shrieked "BAAASTARD!" Moon's head burst in an explosion of stars. He grabbed for the counter as a fog of unconsciousness smothered the light. His knees hit the concrete floor, then his elbows, chest, and head. He could barely hear feet scurrying away into the darkness. Like rat's feet, he thought as he lost consciousness.

★★★

He couldn't have been out for many minutes.

He woke in the utter silence of the blacksmith's shop. Sally was shaking his shoulders.

"What are you doing here?" he asked, straining to keep

her in focus. As he struggled to one knee, he felt the back of his head and found a small knot.

"I followed you, Moon. After you left, it didn't take me long to realize that you could get yourself killed on this stupid quest of yours. I came in through the back way, heard the scuffling in the basement, came down here, and *voila*, here you were, out like a light."

"Skip the clichés, Sally. Did you see who who hit me?"

She shook her head. "He cut and ran when he heard me coming. I saw the old lady upstairs. Is it Tessie Allen?" She was visibly shaken. Her pale skin was pasty, and sweat beaded on her forehead.

"Yes. She's dead."

As Moon stood on shaky legs, Sally watched him anxiously as he struggled to gain his balance, like a newborn calf.

"Don't do this to me any more, Moon. You're way out of your league with this thing." Her hands shook as she guided him by the arm out of the basement.

The light was still on in the archives, and Tessie Allen's body was undisturbed. As he shook his head to clear out the cobwebs, Moon noticed for the first time edges of paper sticking out from beneath her. He gently rolled her over, winced at the vicious welt behind her right ear, and carefully removed the thick stack of paper from her hands. He recognized them as copies of the Stanford Short letters topped by a table of contents, signed at the bottom by Elaine Haskell.

"Wait a minute," he said.

Directly behind them, a copier stood against the wall. He turned it on and copied each one of the sheets in turn. The copier light flashed like a strobe, illuminating the old lady and carving sharp, intermittent shadows out of her body on the floor.

"Moon," said Sally, her cheeks the color of the green walls. "I'm going to be sick."

CHAPTER EIGHTEEN

Sally turned the heat up two degrees on her apartment thermostat. "Moon, this is gruesome. We can't leave that old lady there. I can't believe I let you talk me out of calling the police. You have to, in situations like this."

"No, you don't."

"I'm calling them. Now."

"You do and we'll probably end up in the slammer for a long, long time. Maybe one of us will be discovered strung up to the cell bars, like Mark Keith." He stressed the *us*, and the remark had its desired effect.

Deep furrows creased her worried brow. "You expect me to just sit here and do nothing about it?"

"No, I expect you to help me sift through these," he held up the Short letters, "and see if we can figure out what they mean."

"What will happen to Tessie?"

"Someone will find her. Whoever opens up in the morning."

"And what about the police? Won't they find our fingerprints all over?"

"Yes, and a couple thousand more. Hundreds of people

traipse through the museum every week. Trying to find the
correct set of prints will be damn near impossible. And I was
prescient enough to make copies of the letters and replace the
originals, just in case little Mr. Owen tries to cause trouble.
That could have been him in the museum basement."

She felt the back of his head. "You've got a huge lump
right there. Does it hurt much?"

"Ouch. It hurts, but not too bad."

"Want some ice for it?" Her voice was now soft and sooth-
ing, like a mommy putting a band-aid on a cut knee. He leaned
over and kissed her on the cheek. She accepted it, but her
body stiffened with a tense uneasiness.

"Don't get maudlin on me now," she said. "Are you sure
it was Owen who cracked you on the head?"

"He's the logical suspect. And he probably killed Tessie
Allen, too. The secret to catching him is in these." Moon held
up the thick bundle of papers and fanned them with his thumb,
like his mother used to do with a deck of cards.

"Let me see them," she said. He handed her half the letters and kept half for himself. Sitting on her sofa, they read by
the light of a floor lamp. Moon became entranced by one
spectacular letter written on June 18, 1863, in the trenches
outside Vicksburg:

> Our regiment has been very lucky so far. We have lost two
> killed and five wounded since we have been here in the rear of
> Vicksburg. Our regiment has to go on picket every other night and
> there is not a man but what used from forty to fifty rounds of
> cartridges. So you can judge something of what is going on down
> in Dixie. It is a continual roar of musketry clear around our
> lines—that is fourteen miles and then there are our gun boats and
> mortar fleets throwing shell into the city day and night. Oh you
> ought to see the shell that our mortars throw! It is a splendid
> sight. They throw them two to three miles high over the doomed

city and then they burst and scatter the pieces in every direction. It makes the citizens get into their caves that they have dug into the bluffs. I am in hopes when I write you again Vicksburg will be in our possession. Hiram, when you receive this I want you to sit down and write to me and let me know what you are doing for I am anxious to get letters from Wisconsin. Now don't disappoint me Hiram. I have a good position in Co. H now I think. That is Orderly. I have a good deal to do but that suits me for I like to have something to busy myself about. I shall have to bring this letter to a close. Give my love to Mary and Willie and all the rest of the folks.

I have a magnolia I will put into this letter. Hiram you tell Harriet she owes me a letter. Now be sure and write.
Love, Stannie

Moon held the letter to his nose for a whiff of the magnolia. When he realized it was only a copy of a 128 year old letter, he pulled it away, feeling foolish. He looked over at Sally to see if she had caught him in the act. Fortunately, she was immersed in another letter.

"These letters are marvelous," she said, looking up from the letter. "But I can't help feeling guilty, with Tessie Allen lying there while we read letters. It's macabre."

"I don't feel very good about it, either," Moon said. "But remember, one of Southport's finest has also shown an unhealthy interest in these. Who knows what would happen to us if he found out we had them?"

"Do you think he'd actually hurt us? There are laws against that sort of thing."

"You're damned right he would. Do you know what a throw gun is?"

"No. What is it?"

"It's a term cops use for an untraceable pistol. They throw one down on the ground next to a victim they've gunned down, if they've found out the suspect was unarmed. That way they can claim they shot in self-defense. It's a pretty neat trick, almost always successful, and Manny Edison is an expert with it. He baptized me to the throw gun on my first big story for TheTimes. Some dumb kid had pilfered a box of cookies from a corner grocery store. Edison was cruising the neighborhood and spotted him running out of the store. Manny hopped out of the squad and ran after him and shot him in the back. No warning shot. Just dropped into a three point stance, leveled the pistol and put one right between the kid's shoulder blades. Then he set a throw gun he was carrying in his pocket on the sidewalk next to the kid."

"How do you know all of this?"

"There was a witness. A lady who saw everything from her front window. I was the first reporter on the scene and she told me what she saw. She recanted later, and denied she'd told me anything. Conrad, Jr. wouldn't let me pen one word of it. Said it was unsubstantiated. The gutless bastard."

Moon stared into his cupped hands, like he was reading a crystal ball into the gut-wrenching past. "The kid was thirteen years old, and Edison snuffed him as easily as stepping on a cockroach, Sally. So, do you understand? He doesn't care about what he does, or who he destroys in the process."

"Moon," she cautioned. "I think you should drop this whole thing. You've been shot at, and hit over the head. People are dying all around you. You could be next."

"I owe it to Mark Keith, and now Tessie Allen, to continue."

"In the first place, Keith's death wasn't your fault. And second, you don't even know what you're looking for."

Moon fingered the marble-sized bump behind his ear. "I know it was Owen who whacked me. I can't wait to get my hands on him."

"And what about Manny Edison? What are you going to do with him? And the police? You say it was Owen who was in the Museum, but so were we. We're between a rock and a hard place, Moon."

"I'm going to get help. Tomorrow, I'm going to see Hippo."

She shivered. "That gambler you won the car from? He brushed by me once, and it felt like I'd been licked by a garden slug, on his way to kill some tomato plants. What help could he possibly be?"

Moon laughed at the outrageous simile. "I always said you should write your own column, Sal. But Hippo's smart, and he has a lot of connections. He might be able to keep Edison off my back."

Sally stared at Moon like she'd just seen him for the first time. "Leaving that old lady's corpse in the museum, then copying those letters while she's lying there ... I don't know if I like you any more, Moon. You're a cold man, and now I've unwittingly become your little sidekick in this fiasco. It makes me feel stupid. And unclean."

She rose from the sofa and walked to her bedroom, pausing at the open door. "I don't want anything more to do with this. God forgive me, I won't say anything about what happened at the museum tonight, but I need time to think. You can stay the night. On the sofa." She closed the door behind her.

Upset by her attitude but also anxious to press on, Moon returned to the letters. He was impressed with the strength of young Stanford Short's convictions, his descriptions of the terrible battles, the appalling hardships, and the pathos of the southern civilians as their comfortable world disintegrated before their eyes. In the latter part of 1863, the letters took on a pessimistic tone, and there were increasing references to William Tecumseh Sherman. He recalled that Elaine Haskell believed that Stanford Short might have been Sherman's secretary, and therefore read his mail. The first reference to

Sherman was in a letter dated June, 12, 1863:

Dear Mother and Father,

> *Almost two years have passed since my soldier days began and they seem as though they had been thrown away as far as my present interest is concerned. Yet I hope my presence in the Army has contributed something towards the great object to be gained by the combined effort of thousands of America's sons. I have learned a great deal however, and think my time has not been totally lost.*

> *Your two letters of the 23rd and 24th came on Thursday and have occasioned very much solicitude in regard to Herby's condition. Have anxiously watched for another mail which should bring your daily letter. But no mail steamer has come down since. They say that mail comes but once a week. From your account of Herby's illness I think he must have suffered very much. I hope he is quite recovered by this time. The first week of our life in the field has passed very pleasantly. We have a nice room at General Sherman's headquarters for an office, with an upper room for a bedroom. The General is a large, thin man, with fierce eyes and red hair. He is reticent and keeps much to himself.*

> *Our mess is a poor one, however, which makes us rather dissatisfied with staying here for any length of time. We are to take a steamer in a day or two which will be much more agreeable, as the General will move his headquarters, and we will move with him.*

> *Please forward to Herby my concerns and solicitations.*
> *Love, Stannie*

Later letters indicated that Stanford Short had indeed moved with General Sherman from the western theater through the long march through Georgia.

Moon rose and walked to his coat hanging on Sally's bentwood coat rack at her front door and where he pulled out the letter he'd pilfered from Haskell's house and re-read it: *Owen doesn't think letters are genuine. Barber knows.*

Why would Haskell have written such a truncated note, and to whom? The letters seemed genuine enough to Moon, but he was no historian. And what Barber was Haskell referring to? He stuffed the note back into his shirt pocket and tiptoed into Sally's bedroom. She was on the bed, huddled in a fetal crouch. Ignoring her warning to stay out of her bed, he crawled in beside her and pulled a large afghan over the both of them. He lightly touched her in the small of her back, and she instinctively jerked away. He tossed and turned for half an hour, trying to shake the image of Tessie Allen lying on the archives floor, while Sally groaned in her sleep.

As Tessie's image began to fade, another image intruded into his thoughts: Manny Edison, lurking somewhere in the darkness, waiting, .44 in his outstretched hand, cocked and ready to fire.

CHAPTER NINETEEN

If you took a huge lump of soft, pink clay, punched it down, poked deep holes for eyes, squeezed a small round lump in its middle for a nose, dug out a handful for a mouth and moved that handful below for a fat, shapeless chin, you'd have the beginning of a pretty good likeness of Hippo. Add two shocks of thick brown hair for eyebrows, a wispy moustache, and a hairy brown pot holder on top, and you'd have completed the bust.

The bulk of Hippo's 300-plus pounds had settled comfortably into the seat of his pants. Combined with his ridiculously narrow shoulders, one got the impression of a huge, fleshy pear so wide it needed two bar stools on which to accommodate its prodigious bulges.

Hippo smoked too much, drank too much and ate too much of all the wrong things. His personality was as amoebic as his body, and just when you thought you had him pegged, he would ooze away, leaving behind a fuzzy, impenetrable sensation. There were dark rumors of pederasty, Satanism and worse, but Moon put them off as ignorant gossip by those who couldn't comprehend Hippo's deep intellect.

The grandson of a Greek immigrant who had parlayed a

greengrocer business into a stranglehold of the Dockworkers' local and a healthy slice of Southport's flourishing criminal rackets during Prohibition, Hippo ran a bookmaking operation that took in excess of $30,000 per week on pro sports and track bets, carrying on in the family tradition.

What most of the bettors didn't know—and wouldn't have believed—was that Hippo had a MENSA-sized IQ and a passion for scholarly pursuits, especially Southport history. He was so highly thought of in the intellectual community that he had once written an historical article for the Times.

Moon caught up with him at a mid-morning breakfast break, one of about a dozen meals he consumed daily, at the lunch counter at Biddle's Drugs, a seven story 1870s cream city brick building located a few blocks from the Southport Times offices at the north end of the Civic Center Mall.

The drugstore occupied the first floor of the building, and various offices occupied about half the rooms on the remaining floors. In the 1970s the Southport City Council had approved sealing off the downtown's main street into an open air mall. By banishing autos and planting a few scattered, anemic trees, the Council had deluded themselves into thinking they had created a Mid-American version of an Italian piazza, bustling with commerce. But what they actually accomplished was to accelerate the death throes of the central business district and drive most of the shops to new shopping centers on the city's edge, or out of business. Biddle's Drugs was one of the few stubborn holdouts, kept in business more by its old-fashioned lunch counter than the pharmacist behind his counter in the rear of the store.

Wiry Old Man Biddle, proprietor of the drug store, was working the griddle under a sign on white board with big red and blue letters that read Biddle's Griddle, frying two hot dogs split down the middle. He concentrated on the crackling dogs as they sputtered on the hot grill and tried not to think about his wife Sammy. They'd been married 30 years and that morning, for the first time in their married life, she had rolled away from him, putting her elbow over her breast to prevent him from touching her. He couldn't imagine what he'd done to make her feel that way, and he was worried.

Hippo dumped three level teaspoons of sugar into his coffee, stirring vigorously. "So what's on your mind?" he asked Moon.

"Tell me about Elaine Haskell, Hippo."

"Elaine Haskell was a tyrant and a bitch. She knew her history, but she always bet against the line. Got her markers for five hundred bucks. Lot of good that'll do me now."

Moon slipped him the sheet of paper he'd pilfered from Elaine Haskell's house. "You know a guy named Barber?"

"Where'd you swipe this?"

"What makes you think I swiped it?"

"After taking your poker money for years, I know a little bit about you, Moon. There's a bit of Fagin in your heart. I don't think you've ever quite shed your corner Chicago saloon upbringing."

"Hey. I put Chicago behind me twenty years ago ...except for my old man's funeral, I've never been back. My childhood's not the issue here."

"Everyone's childhood is always the issue. Read your Freud."

"Do you know a guy named Barber?"

Hippo pointed at the paper. "That's Elaine's handwriting. I recognize it. But I don't know anybody named Barber. The first sentence intrigues me, though. I suppose the reference to 'the letters' means the Stanford Short letters?"

"It does."

"And Owen doubts their authenticity? That's curious."

"Why?"

"Local gossips say Owen leaked the news about their discovery. Elaine was furious with him. She wanted to research the letters and have everything tied into a neat package before she released them to the public—in book form, I would imagine, with her name and photo prominently displayed on the cover and news releases mailed to all the media. She was a ruthless self-promoter, and a pompous ass. Have you seen the letters?"

Biddle set two hotdogs, wrapped in bacon, topped with melted cheese and nestled in soft white buns, in front of Hippo, who then squeezed ketchup on them and proceeded to inhale them. "This is about the only place you can still get a real francheesie," he said, talking around the food stuffed in his mouth. "In California, they'd take a place like this, put in ferns, a brass rail, call the francheesie a 'le hot dog de fromage,' charge five bucks for it, and serve it with Perrier or a wine spritzer."

Moon watched in awe as the gambler shoved the other half of the dog into his cavernous kisser, chomped three times and swallowed.

"It's why I love Southport, Moon. Time has passed us by in a lot of ways, and that isn't all bad. Here you can still find places like Biddle's—a real drugstore with a real lunch counter. Hell, so many other American cities are wrapped up in redevelopment, that they knock down their historic buildings, their most important assets, all in the name of progress. And then when they've finished, they try to re-create what they had in the first place. It ends up looking like a poor-man's Disneyworld."

"No argument from me, Hippo."

"Damn right," he grunted, dabbing daintily at the corners of his mouth with a paper napkin. "Now, tell me. Have you seen the letters?"

"Yes. I've got copies."

"How'd you manage that?"

"I've got my ways."

He wagged a fat finger. "See what I mean about Fagin? By the way, what makes you think Barber is a man? It could be a woman."

"It's a possibility."

"Where are you heading with all this?"

"What do you mean?"

"You obviously don't believe that poor bastard who stretched his neck in the hoosegow killed the illustrious Miz Haskell, do you?"

"No, I don't. And I think I know who did kill her—and Tessie Allen, too. But I need help. Qualified help."

"I'll give you some good advice. Drop it. The suspect is dead. The case is closed. This is a no-win situation, Moon, and I'd hate to see you come to a violent end. I enjoy taking your football bets. They keep me in hotdogs."

Moon ignored the crack. "So, can you help me?"

"I could thumb through a few books, I suppose, but let me make you another offer. My brother-in-law, Karl Von Essen, is an expert on the Civil War; he could examine the letters, check for their authenticity and tell you just how valuable they are."

"Why can't you do that?"

"I've got an ulterior motive. Karl is an extremely competent but unambitious historian teaching part time at Saint Ignatious. If he could somehow become involved in the publishing of the Stanford Short letters, it would go a long way toward securing his tenure at the college. That would also create a more secure future for my sister and little nephew."

"I didn't know you had family, Hippo."

"Not many people do. They prefer to see me as an overweight satyr with a mysterious and dissolute past. Let them think what they want; it enhances my business. Could you work with my brother-in-law?"

"Sure. Why not? But let's keep this on the QT. The case has an added dimension."

"Like Manny Edison?"

Moon raised his eyebrows in surprise. "Yes, like Manny Edison. Somehow he's involved himself in the investigation— sort of a freelance thing."

"Manny Edison is more than an added dimension, Moon. I'd suggest you get some protection." He reached into his coat pocket and pulled out a snub-nosed .38 and slid it across the counter to Moon. Old Man Biddle stared impassively at the gun and turned back to flipping eggs.

"Don't look shocked, Moon," Hippo snorted. "Tools of the trade. Gambling is a business based on luck. I'm a gambler. This is my lucky gun. Take it."

"Guns make me nervous."

"No. *Other* men with guns should make you nervous. Men like Manny Edison."

"I'll pass."

He shrugged and shoved the gun back into his pocket. "How about Dean, then?" he said, nodding over at "Mean Dean" Paskewicz sitting at the end of the counter, reading a dog-eared copy of *Sports Illustrated*. Paskewicz looked up and nodded condescendingly to Moon. Moon noticed the bulge of Paskewicz's tattooed biceps as he turned the magazine's pages.

A for-hire bodyguard, Paskewicz was a former state Golden Gloves champ who'd spent ten years on the pro boxing meat circuit. He'd won 33 of his 54 fights, garnering a busted nose that spread across his face, and two cauliflower ears as trophies of his pro career. His last fight had been against Teddy Nixon, a 250-pound animal who'd boxed his way out of Joliet Prison. Nixon had broken Paskewicz's cheek with a round-house right in the fourth round of the six-rounder. Paskewicz had stuck out the remaining two rounds, taking uncountable brutal body shots as he kept his fists up to protect what remained of his face. The fight ended his mediocre career, leaving him penniless, with a busted cheek that never quite healed and a perpetually runny nose.

"You've got problems, Hippo? Is that why Dean's babysitting you?" asked Moon.

Hippo stared at Paskiewicz. "No, no problems. I like to let him tag along once in a while. It makes him happy." Moon thought he read something other than brotherly love in the gambler's look. "It's in my best interests to have you stay healthy, Moon. I don't have to remind you that you had a hundred dollars on your Bears the other day. That makes nine hundred you owe me. You want to settle up?"

"I'm a little light right now. Give me two weeks."

"I'll take the Rambler back. Wipe the slate clean."

"Fat chance."

"You're lucky that I'm fond of you. Otherwise, I might settle the debt with a broken bone or two." He said it loud enough for Paskewicz to hear. Mean Dean looked up from the magazine and grinned at Moon, eyes flat and expressionless as two black buttons. Hippo laughed from deep in the pit of his stomach. "It's why I carry markers, Moon. Other bookies, they want the cash. I prefer paper. Paper is my hammer over society."

"Well, keep my hammer in your pocket for another week or two, Hippo. Give me your brother-in-law's address." Hippo wrote it down for him while Moon paid for the coffee and dogs.

"See ya, Moon," said Mean Dean, chuckling menacingly as Moon walked past him and out the door. He sniffed and wiped a finger under his nose.

Old Man Biddle watched the yolks harden on the eggs on the griddle, wondering if his fifty-year-old wife had found herself a boyfriend.

CHAPTER TWENTY

Sheridan Road, which connects Chicago and Green Bay, was once the main drag for the Chicago-Milwaukee corridor. Over the years, as interstate highways were constructed, Sheridan Road lost its importance but still carried substantial traffic shuttling between Chicago and Milwaukee and the midsized cities between.

Karl Von Essen's home was off the east side—the lake side—of Sheridan Road, north of Southport, down a narrow gravel road lined with tall oaks blanketed in snow. Moon strained to read addresses on the roadside mailboxes as he cruised slowly by the houses. He finally found Von Essen's at the end of the road that dead-ended a few feet from a bluff fifty feet above Lake Michigan's icy waters. The lake had been eating away at the shoreline for centuries, taking a hundred feet or more in certain areas. On the city's south side, the lake had gotten really aggressive and pulled in a half dozen houses as it chewed into the shoreline. Moon remembered driving down the lake shore road in the Rambler with Sally, who oohed and aahed like a school girl every time they passed a house slumping into the lake, ripped off its foundation by the powerful waves.

Von Essen had tried to stem the lake's advance by dumping rocks, branches and assorted fill down the side of the bluff. It was an exercise in futility. If the lake wanted to swallow Von Essen's property, nothing would stop it, least of all sticks and stones. As Moon knocked on Von Essen's front door, he watched the rapacious waves gnaw at the fragile shoreline and thought about what Sally had said about his being cold, wondering if he could narrow the gap that seemed to be widening between them.

The man who answered was small and grub-worm white. He wore a huge purple sweater, blue sweat pants and fuzzy socks with holes in the toes. His hair was blond and unkempt, his eyes red-rimmed, and he had a Kirk Douglas cleft in his chiseled jaw.

"I'm Karl Von Essen. You're Moon, right?" He shook Moon's hand enthusiastically and pulled him into the oven-hot living room.

The house was comfortably messy. Books littered the floor. A sofa and two brown vinyl recliners were covered with hand-knit afghans, and on one of the recliners, a year-old baby with golden ringlets toyed with a ring of colorful oversized plastic keys, goo-gooing as he shoved them into his mouth and kicked his chubby piston-like legs.

Von Essen motioned Moon to the unoccupied recliner. "Sit," he commanded. The baby dropped his keys and stared, goggle-eyed, at Moon. Bubbles of spittle ringed its lips.

Moon handed Von Essen the Stanford Short letters. "Hippo said you were something of an expert on the Civil War."

"It's my passion." He riffled through the letters quickly, then paused to study them more closely. After fifteen minutes, he looked up at Moon and his eyes brightened. "These are terrific!" he pronounced.

"You think so?"

"This is quite a find. Marvelous. Marvelous." His enthusiasm was infectious. The baby picked up the plastic keys again and shoved them into his mouth, gurgling happily, like his daddy. "I heard about these. It was a poorly-kept secret among archivists that Elaine had discovered them."

"So they're significant?"

"Oh, yes. They certainly are."

"Enough to kill for?"

"What?"

"Three people have died, probably because of those letters. Do they provide a motive for murder?"

"At first glance, no. They're a find, no doubt about that, but only of local interest. Where are the originals?"

"At the Society. Will you look at these? Maybe you can find something that would help me clear the name of an innocent man."

"I'll do what I can, of course, but I doubt that I'll find anything."

"I'll pay you for your time."

Von Essen took pity on Moon's obvious frustration. "Don't bother, time is what I have plenty of. As you can see," he waved an arm, gesturing at the messy room, "I'm Mister Mom. My wife works outside the home as a kindergarten teacher. I work here."

"History?"

"Yes and no. History's my avocation and my passion. I write book reviews, speeches for executives, anything to bring in a buck. I also teach a course in American history at Saint Ignatious."

"So you're a writer?"

"Not in your class, of course. I'd like to write a newspaper column, though."

"It's not such a big deal, believe me. A little bit of notoriety for mouthing off in print."

"It's steady work, and that makes the difference. I could

care less if it was in a newspaper or written in chalk on the sidewalk. All I'd like is a steady paycheck. It would keep my wife off my back." He looked over his shoulder toward what Moon assumed to be a bedroom door, as if his wife would storm out at any moment, rolling pin in hand.

Moon wasn't in the mood to hear Von Essen relate his marital difficulties, and he got up to leave. "You'll give the letters a good look?"

"I'll give them more than that. These are like candy for me. I'll call you tomorrow if I find anything."

The baby had fallen asleep, a thin line of drool hanging down one corner of his mouth, the plastic keys clutched tightly in his fat little fist.

CHAPTER TWENTY-ONE

Driving soothed Moon, and helped him to think. He cruised through the seemingly deserted Southport; first through the southeast area, where the big homes near the lake tended to be overweight and self-important—a lot like their owners— to the small, neat working-class bungalows on the north side, and then into the decaying center of town, where tired two and three flats mingled with small factories and distributor- ships. The snow seemed to be a darker shade of gray here as it drifted between junk cars jacked up and left for dead on the narrow streets.

The city's center was also home to larger factories and foundries—some well over one hundred years old—where everything from autos to lawn mower engines were made. Most of the buildings were hulking, low-slung and pock- marked brick with bars over the windows and sawtooth roofs. Across from each factory were two or three drab taverns, where the work-weary could get boilermakers and chili and take in a Sunday football game, play a few rounds of cribbage or a game of eight ball and argue politics. They were tough men, and a few tough women who frequented these joints: grease stains under fingernails, calloused hands, hair rough-combed.

But they pulled down good money, enough to make it worthwhile to enter the dungeon-like factories eight hours a day, five days a week, time-and-a-half for overtime.

With the sudden bankruptcy of the city's largest employer, the American Auto Works, all that was now disappearing. Moon cruised by the enormous abandoned auto plant, once home to 20,000 workers, now a casualty of global competition, as a half-dozen huge cranes hammered away at the ancient brick. One small bulldozer with pinching arms like a pop-riveted land crab reached up, grabbed ten-foot lengths of metal support beams, neatly snipped them at the ends and dumped them in a pile for salvagers to cart off. Later, they would be melted down and recast as new beams for new factories halfway around the world.

The dozers and cranes slowly peeled the factory apart, brick by brick, beam by beam, while a knot of onlookers stood dumbly on the sidewalk outside the chain-link fence surrounding the demolition site—bored jackals watching lions savage their kill. A scattering of small fires burned inside the site, raising thick clouds of smoke into the bright winter sky, obscuring the midday sun.

Depressed by the sight of the dying factory, Moon steered the Rambler out of the city and toward the small lakes and resort towns in the western end of the county.

★★★

At 7:00 AM, Moon pulled the Rambler into the residents' lot for the Hotel Nelson and trudged over the unshoveled sidewalks to the hotel lobby. Sam was working the front desk, which meant there were only a few coffee hounds in the restaurant, pouring their own brew, arguing about the Super Bowl. The subject bored Moon. Once the Bears were eliminated, football season held no interest for him.

"Look what the cat dragged in." Sam winked, forcing a

smile. Moon had been out all night, and Sam figured he'd spent it with a woman. In actuality, Moon had driven all the way into the next county, then turned around and made it halfway home before he'd pulled over on the side of the road. He'd huddled under a blanket in his front seat and caught four hours of sleep before being wakened at daybreak by a sheriff's deputy who had rapped on his window and told him to move along.

Now Moon had a stiff neck and a bad attitude and he wasn't up for Sam's locker-room patter. "Any messages?" he asked.

"One. Some guy named Vanessa. My old man named me that, I'd kill him."

"You mean Von Essen?"

"Maybe that's it. I wrote it down." He handed Moon a slip of paper with an unreadable scribble on it.

"Can you translate this for me? I left the code book in my room," said Moon.

Sam yanked the paper out of his hand. "It says 'come over as soon as you can. I've got exciting news.' You can't read that?"

But Moon was already out the door and on his way to Karl Von Essen's house.

CHAPTER TWENTY-TWO

V̇on Essen answered the door on the first knock, wearing the same baggy purple sweater and blue sweatpants. His eyes were red and his face flushed, as though he'd been up all night.

"I've got some pretty exciting news," he said. Moon looked around for the little baby with the plastic keys, but he was nowhere to be seen. Von Essen sat on the sofa, Stanford Short letters in hand. Moon sat next to him.

"Know much about the Civil War?" Von Essen asked.

"I just saw *Glory*. I thought it was a great film."

"Me too. But that was just a tiny snippet of what was going on then. Suffice it to say there has never been a more bloody, more divisive, yet more exciting time in American history. And what we've got here"—he held up the copies of the letters—"is a first-hand account of someone who was very close to one of the main movers and shakers of that period."

"Stanford Short was Sherman's secretary?"

"No, he wasn't. But his correspondence—after the beginning of the march through Georgia—suggests he read the General's mail. There's too much detailed evidence in the letters—troop movements, dispositions of artillery, and the like—to suggest anything otherwise."

"You're saying that Stanford Short read Sherman's mail?"

"I think he did, yes."

"And does that fact make the letters worth killing for?"

"No. It would have raised their historical value somewhat, but not to that degree."

"What *are* you telling me, Von Essen?"

"Karl, please."

"Ok, Karl. Now explain."

He handed Moon the sheets indexing the letters' chronological order.

"Look at that."

"I'm looking."

"Don't you see?"

"No, I don't. What is it that I'm supposed to be looking for?"

Karl ran his finger down the second sheet. "The boy wrote home without fail at least once a week, see?" Moon followed Karl's finger as it coursed slowly down the paper. "From the beginning of the war to the very end, he wrote to his parents like clockwork." Karl's finger stopped at the end of the page. "Except for here. For some reason, there's a break of one month. He stops on March twenty-eight, eighteen sixty-five, and doesn't resume until April twenty-nine, eighteeen sixty-five, which I assume was his last letter home."

Moon recalled the obituary Tessie Allen had given him. "That was the day he was killed," he said. "That break in the letters—wasn't that after the war ended?"

"It was early April when Lee surrendered, yes. But there were still substantial Confederate forces in the field. In fact, Sherman was in the process of negotiating a truce with General Joseph Johnston around the time of the break in Stanford Short's letters."

Karl continued, "Remember that Lincoln had been assas-

sinated by that time. The federal government was controlled
by Secretary of War Stanton, who wanted to make the South
pay for the crime of waging war on the Union. Sherman had
offered generous peace terms to Johnston, and that sent Stanton
up the wall. He called Sherman every name in the book—
including traitor—and he had friends in the press to help
him. They hated Sherman, and he hated them in return, once
suggesting that reporters in the field be shot as spies. He felt
that their dispatches aided and abetted the enemy."

"Still a topical subject," said Moon.

"In many cases, he was right. Reporters did telegraph his
troop movements and caused many unneeded Union casual-
ties." He sat back, thumbing through the letters. "Let me read
this letter to you," he said. "It's the most important one among
them. But first, let me give you some background." Moon
saw a savage fire in Von Essen's eyes, like someone who had
unearthed a gold doubloon in his back yard, and wanted to
tear up the earth for miles around, looking for more.

"On March twenty-seven, eighteen sixty-five, Sherman
met with Grant, Admiral David Porter and President Lincoln
at City Point, Virginia," Von Essen said. "They met on the steam-
boat River Queen. They discussed how to go about ending
the war, as it was obvious by then that they were going to
win. Your boy Stanford Short was there. For evidence, I'd like
to read you this letter." He pulled a pair of round bifocals
from his shirt pocket, balanced them on the bridge of his
nose, and began to read:

> City Point, Virginia, March 28, 1865.
> Dear Father.
> I have finally met him, the great man, Mr. Lincoln, the
> defender of our Republic and our Union. He has come to meet
> with General Sherman and General Grant and Admiral David
> Porter. None of us know what it is all about, but it must be

something of great import, to bring these powerful personages together in one room. As for Mr. Lincoln, I saw him alone, in a room on a riverboat docked here in the city. There was no elegance about him, no elegance in him. He was plainly clad in a suit of black, that illy fitted him. No fault of his tailor, however. Such a figure could not be fitted. He was tall and lean, and as he sat in a folded up sort of way, one would have almost thought him deformed. It was at first a shock to me to think that this plain figure was the President of our Great Republic, but he saw me and smiled, and in that smile I saw the inner greatness within the man.

How is mother?

"There are a few more lines inquiring about the folks back home," he said. "What do you think of it?"

"Interesting," Moon replied. "But what does it mean?"

"It means that our boy was very close to Sherman. He met Lincoln, and in all probability, Grant."

"And?"

"And that there are a series of missing Short letters, between March twenty-nine, and April twenty-eight, eighteen sixty-five. Those may be what your two historians died for."

Moon pointed at the letters on Von Essen's lap. "I thought these were what I'd been looking for. Now you're telling me that there are additional missing letters?"

"As sure as I can be about anything."

"What could be in them?"

"If I were to hazard a guess, I'd say something political. Like I said, during that time, General Sherman had it out with Stanton and the rest of the reconstructionists. A lot of accusations and counter-accusations were bandied about. Perhaps Stanford Short heard something or saw something important and wrote home about it."

"Like what?"

"I don't know, but I do know there are missing letters. Four, maybe more."

"And those letters could be the motive behind the murders?"

"If they were hot enough, they could be."

Moon knew the evidence was flimsy, but at least he finally had a qualified opinion that the letters might be the motive for the murders. But how in the hell had Edison known about them? Had Owen tipped him off? And what was in them to make Edison want them so badly?

Moon was beginning to doubt who had dispatched the two old ladies.

CHAPTER TWENTY-THREE

1865

Stanford Short wandered back through camp to his room. The stars were out in full force, and the night sky looked like it was shot full of holes.

"I have to admit," he mumbled. "I'm a bit drunk." He laughed at that, remembering when he'd signed up, and Charlie Fay and he had created a manifesto for the troops at Camp Henry. They had formed the 'Southport Temperance Alliance,' and its members took an oath of loyalty to the Union, death to all who would destroy the Union and abstinence from alcoholic beverages. Only fifty of the eleven hundred men in camp had signed the manifesto. Short thought about the strongly worded, idealistic paper he and Fay had drafted. They had been so damned high-minded in those days—like two babes in the woods. Short wondered what his temperate father would think if he saw him now, stumbling drunk into his room, falling onto his bed in full uniform.

"Sorry, Pa," he muttered as he drifted off into deep sleep. His last thoughts before oblivion were of Charlie Fay, hard liquor, and a fine brass band serenading the General.

★★★

Meriwether Pickens had followed Captain Short from the

camp, always keeping a safe distance, and watched as Short stumbled into the headquarters mansion. Pickens sneaked around behind the big house, which was lightly guarded, because of the end of hostilities two days before, and entered through the kitchen door. The house was quiet, except for voices coming from a room down near the front of the house. Pickens thought he recognized Sherman's voice and laugh, others picking up the cue and laughing with him.

"Go ahead and laugh, boy-o," whispered Pickens. In a few minutes, he would have the damning letter and he, Meriwether Pickens, would be wealthy. The first thing he'd do when he mustered out and got back to Southport would be to piss on Stanford Short's boot. He thought about Short's beautiful younger sister Elaine and licked his chops. He wouldn't piss on her boot. No-siree. He'd tend to her, too, but in a different way.

Pickens tiptoed down the long main hall and then another hall that led to Short's small room. The captain was stretched out prone on his small bed, one arm flung out, snoring loudly. Pickens could smell the cheap bourbon Short had shared with Fay and the other men around the campfire. He caressed the navy Colt stuck in his waistband, and then pulled it out and leveled it at the space between Short's eyes. Just a gentle squeeze of the trigger and Short's brains would be plastered on the wall. Later, he thought. First, get the letter. He began to silently search the room, going through every inch of Short's traps, through the drawers of Short's small writing desk, anywhere the letter could have been hidden.

Pickens was down on his knees, peering under Short's bed, when he heard footsteps approaching from down the hall. He quickly rolled under the bed and watched as a pair of black, shiny boots and a pair of scuffed shoes entered the room.

"Stannie?" a voice whispered.

Sherman! The old man hisself, right here in Short's room,

Pickens thought.

"Whew! It smells like a brewery in here!" said the man in the boots.

Pickens didn't recognize the voice of Brigadier General Alpheus S. "Ol' Pap" Williams, leader of Sherman's XX Corps, a dull old man who loved good whisky and fought a losing battle with gout. A lawyer and judge before the war, Williams had proven himself to be an able commander when the fighting got hot and heavy.

"You want me to wake him?" asked Williams, as he moved closer to the bed. Pickens nervously fingered the pistol in his belt again. He didn't want to shoot no damned generals, but he would, by God, if he had to. The boots stopped a few feet from the bed.

"No," said Sherman. "Let him sleep, Pap. The boy's been through hell."

"We all have, Uncle Billy," said Williams softly.

"That we have," said Sherman. "But this boy ..." His voice drifted off. Staring at the dead-drunk Short, Sherman mused on the probability that the boy might have read and deliberately destroyed the foolish letter that he had written in such haste the day before. It would have been right in character with the intensely loyal and overly-protective Short. If Grant or Stanton had seen such an indiscreet letter ...The General shuddered visibly.

"What's wrong?" asked Williams, noticing Sherman's discomfort.

Sherman shrugged off the question. "Nothing," he said.

"Headquarters is pulling out tonight," said Williams. "Is your boy coming along?"

"No," sighed Sherman. "I've allowed him to stay on for another day. A friend of his just came in with his regiment, the First Wisconsin. The two of them have a lot to talk about. Headquarters' wagons and the Seventeenth Corps leave tonight for Virginia. We go to Savannah, then on to Wilmington and Hilton Head. Stannie will meet us there. Let's go now. Leave him to his dreams."

Pickens watched as they left the room, and he breathed a sigh of relief and crawled out from under the bed. He had searched every inch of the room and found no letter. Short must have somehow gotten the letter off home, he thought. He cursed as he thought of the letter now on its way to Southport, out of his reach.

Pickens pulled the pistol from his belt, put the barrel against Short's temple, and pulled the hammer back. "Some day, boy-o," he hissed. He uncocked the pistol, put it back into his belt, and slipped out of the room to return to the woods. Now that he knew that Short no longer had the letter, Pickens had no reason to let him live. Tomorrow, he thought. I'll do it tomorrow.

Pickens found a group of Indiana volunteers around a campfire and joined them to split the remains of a jug of corn liquor, passing out at the edge of the fire an hour before dawn.

CHAPTER TWENTY-FOUR
1991

Moon nosed the Rambler behind Manny Edison's sleek black sports car. After a couple of blocks, he realized Edison was following a bright red late-model Ford Escort.

Edison maneuvered through traffic like a shark through a school of unwary fish. The Ford took a right turn. Edison followed, and Moon followed him. The Ford turned into a driveway adjacent to home with dingy yellow asbestos siding. Edison parked in front of the home, but he left the engine running. Moon turned down a side street and parked out of sight, where he watched Edison watch the home. The cop lit a cigarette, puffed slowly for ten minutes, then he flicked it out the car window, pulled out from curb and drove away.

Moon swung around the corner and parked in front of the house. He walked to the front door and knocked, curious who would answer. An elderly woman opened the door. "I'm not buying anything," she said defensively.

"Don't I know you from somewhere?" Moon said. "Do you work at the Historical Society?"

"Yes, I do." She poked her nose forward and squinted through her glasses. "Do I know you?"

Moon finally made the connection. "You're the lady who interrupted my conversation with Tessie Allen the other day, aren't you? Hazel, I think, she called you."

"Yes. I'm Hazel Fine. I remember you. And you're the man from the newspaper who kept pestering Tessie. What do you want?"

"I'm investigating Tessie's murder. For the newspaper."

"She was my best friend."

"Then it must have come as even more of a shock to you."

"It was a terrible shock." Hazel looked like she was about to cry.

Moon patted her gently on the hand. "May I come in?" he asked. She opened the door and he stepped inside. The house was cluttered with Victoriana: dozens of knick-knacks of all kinds covering every tabletop and every bit of available floor space. There were diminutive ceramic figurines in 18th century costumes, men bowing to ladies, ladies curtseying in return; tiny milk maids, bent over their buckets; a plaster circus strongman, grimacing as he tugged on his plaster barbells; and animals of all descriptions—tigers, fish, birds, and a large gray plaster elephant frozen in stride next to an old television.

Moon ran a finger across the top of the TV. "Jeez," he said in amazement. "A Muntz television. My pa bought us a Muntz when I was six years old. Does it still work?"

"Of course it does," she said as she took off her coat and hung it in a closet. She didn't offer to take his coat. "It's the first and only television I've ever owned. I don't watch much TV—Lawrence Welk, some public television. I prefer radio. Would you like some herb tea?"

"Tea will be fine, thank you. I like old movies," Moon said as she left the room to brew the tea.

"So do I," she said from the kitchen. "What's your favorite?" Her teapot began to whistle.

"*The Searchers*, with John Wayne."

She carried in two delicate flower-patterned cups and a matching tea pot on a tray and set them on top of the television between two Hummell figurines.

"Too macho for me," she said. "I prefer anything with Ginger Rogers and Fred Astaire. Milk, sugar or lemon?"

Moon hadn't had tea in years, and he couldn't remember exactly what went with it, so he said yes to all three. She put nothing in hers.

They stood by the television, slowly sipping. Moon made a face. The brew tasted like boiled branches and leaves. "Tell me about Harold Owen," he asked.

"Harold Owen was a nice little boy who went astray."

"How so?"

"His mother and father—especially his father—tried to steer him into an industrial career. He would have none of it. Harold pursued scholarly interests—the arts and sciences."

"And mom and dad didn't like it?"

"Oh, heavens no! Did you know Sullivan Owen?"

"Not really. I'm originally from Chicago, but I've heard of him, of course."

"Well, everything you've heard is true. He was a brilliant man, an inventive genius. But he was ruthless. He had hoped Harold would be mechanically inclined, like his he was. Harold was a great disappointment to Sullivan Owen. And to Lydia, as well."

"Lydia?"

"His mother. You've never met her, I take it?"

"No. Never."

"If you ever do, you'll certainly remember her. She makes an indelible impression"

"Tell me more about Harold. And Elaine Haskell."

"Elaine was given the executive directorship of the Society ten years ago," she said as she poured herself another cup of tea.

Moon refused a second, holding a hand over his cup. "Lydia Owen was livid. Harold took it in stride, though. He did his best to work around Elaine, which isn't easy. She's a terror to work with."

"You mean she *was* a terror," he corrected.

"Yes, of course. Harold and Elaine had a standoffish relationship, but the Society prospered. We have over a thousand members now, you know. Anyway, everything seemed to come unraveled after the Stanford Short letters were discovered."

"How so?"

"Harold and Elaine had a horrible fight over them. I never did get all the facts straight, but rumor has it that it was actually Harold who discovered the letters, while Elaine took the credit."

"That would tick me off."

"Well, it ticked off Harold, let me tell you." She peeked coyly over the rim of her teacup. She was flirting with him, he thought. There was a flush of excitement in her cheeks.

"How about Tessie Allen?" Moon asked.

"Tessie and I were best friends. We grew up together. In fact, we were born on the same day: the Fourth of July, nineteen-eleven. We went to the same schools. We even dated the same boys, although I married and Tessie stayed single. I never could understand why. She was such a beautiful woman. We used to go to the movies—the Orpheum—it's abandoned now, every Saturday night, and the boys would just flock around her." Her eyes filled with tears. "And now she's gone. Just like that."

"Did she have any sort of relationship with Harold Owen?" Moon wanted to stop Hazel from wallowing too deeply in the past.

"Relationship?"

"I mean, did she know him well?"

"Of course she did! She worked with him. And her father

worked for his father. Tessie's father was his chief engineer.
Sullivan Owen may have been brilliant, but without John Allen,
he would have never managed to make it in the business
world."

"It all seems so close—almost family, you could say."

"You can. And you should. The city was ruled by a dozen
or so very influential families from the 19th century right up
until the end of the Second World War. With Tessie gone, Lydia
Owen is the only survivor of those illustrious clans. It's funny,
but when we were young, if you had asked me who would
outlive all the rest, I would have said Lydia Owen."

"How about you? You seem to be alive and kicking."

"Oh, I am that. But I never was a member of her circle."
She held up a hand, stopping him before he could speak. "I
know what you're going to say, but Tessie was different from
the rest. She was my friend because she liked me, not because
I moved in her social circle. My father ran a shoe store. It's
still there, but it's boarded up now. Has been for years." She
sighed again and set her teacup down on top of the television. "That's all there is, really."

"Do you think that Harold Owen would have had Elaine
Haskell killed because of the Stanford Short letters?"

"Harold Owen? Kill Elaine?" She paused, giving what she
obviously considered an outrageous thought time to digest.

"I don't think so," she finally said. "But you're right about
one thing." She glanced furtively over her shoulder and then
edged closer to Moon. "Tessie was killed because she discovered something," she whispered conspiratorially. Moon could
smell lilac on her breath. He wondered if she gargled with
her perfume. "Something about those letters. I know she
wanted to tell me about it. She hinted at it. But she was too
afraid."

"Afraid of what?"

"I don't know. But after Elaine was murdered–" She

paused, as if holding in a terrible secret.

"Have you told the police your suspicions?"

"Yes. But they weren't interested in what I had to say."

All except Manny Edison, Moon thought. He knew the importance of the Short letters. Which is why he had been following Hazel Fine. He imagined the cop coiling his hands around her aged neck, like a snake around a mouse, slowly tightening as she vainly clawed at his fingers. A melodramatic image, but probably close to the mark.

Hazel's eyes brimmed with tears. "I can't help thinking about Tessie. Who would have thought anyone would murder such a sweet woman?"

Moon set his teacup down and said goodbye. He didn't want to share any more of her past or anguish over her future. It made him feel uneasy, as if he were peeking into someone's coffin.

CHAPTER TWENTY-FIVE

Moon was exhausted and incensed as he marched up the walk to the front door of Owen's home. He wished the entire business were over.

Owen's home was an impressive four-story Georgian brick. With countless windows and a heavy front door only slightly smaller than the entrance to a medieval castle, it was large enough to intimidate all but the boldest solicitors.

Moon grabbed the door's ornate brass knocker and rapped three times. Lights began to flick on upstairs, and then Moon heard the patter of feet scurrying toward the front door and hands fumbling at the lock.

When the door opened, it revealed the diminutive Mr. Owen—tousle-haired, tugging a bathrobe around his slight frame, nudging his glasses up the bridge of his nose, obviously displeased at the identity of his visitor and the lateness of the hour.

"Goodnight," he said curtly, attempting to shut the door in Moon's face. Moon quickly wedged his toe between the door and its frame.

"Hold on," he said as he pushed at the door. His foot was beginning to hurt, and Owen was stronger than expected.

Moon had to use both hands to force the door open.

"Must I call the police?" Owen said.

"Please do. Then you and I can talk to them about the missing letters."

Owen let go of the door abruptly, and none too soon. Moon's arms were beginning to throb.

Owen pulled his robe tighter and retied the belt, trying to maintain an air of nonchalance. "What missing letters?"

"Stanford Short's letters. There are a few of them missing, aren't there?"

Owen casually smoothed his night-rumpled hair and pushed his glasses up again. "Who told you that?" he said. "You couldn't have learned that on your own."

"Thanks for the compliment. I had an historian friend look at them. He found a big hole in their sequence, where there should have been more letters. Four, maybe more, he says."

"This historian friend of yours, is he qualified?"

"I think so. What's more, I think I know who's got the missing letters."

Owen stepped back and motioned with his arm. "Come in," he said.

Moon stepped into a large foyer dominated by a mammoth crystal chandelier. To the left there was a dining room with a long, shiny mahogany Queen Anne table flanked by eight matching chairs, and to the right was a large living room with two sofas, several end tables and a half-dozen plush armchairs arranged precisely on the polished oak floors. Both rooms had large, almost walk-in fireplaces on their west walls and twelve foot ceilings decorated with cherrywood beams. Moon faced a wide staircase covered with an oriental runner secured by shining brass rods. Halfway to the second floor, it took a sharp curve at a small landing where three windows were strategically placed to catch the evening sunlight.

Moon was interested in hearing what Owen had to say about himself. "How is it an historian can afford a place like this?"

"My father was Sullivan Owen."

Harold Owen was smugly secure that this explained everything, but Moon feigned ignorance. "He was a big name a long time ago, wasn't he?"

Owen sighed impatiently. "Not so long ago. He created the prototype of the four wheel drive truck."

"So he made a lot of money, right?"

"Yes, he did."

"And he left it to you?"

"Yes. To Mother and me."

"Your mother is still alive?"

"Yes, very much so," he said, irritated.

"And Daddy left you comfortable enough to pursue your hobby."

"History is not my hobby, Mr. Moon. It is my vocation."

"Oh, sure. But historians can't really afford a home like this, can they?"

"Have you come here to discuss the Stanford Short letters, or dissect my life history?"

"Aren't you going to invite me inside?"

"You are inside."

"I mean past the foyer?"

"No. Now tell me what you know about the missing letters."

"I know that Stanford Short was very close to Sherman, and that Elaine Haskell knew it. I know that Short was with Sherman up to the very end of the war. I know he wrote home diligently—once a week—and that there was a break in the series of letters. And I know that in all probability those letters may contain some pretty significant historical information. Enough to get two people murdered, and cause one suicide."

"You said you thought you knew who has the letters. Do you mind telling me who?"

Looking to rattle what he thought was Owen's staged indifference, Moon handed him the note he'd found in Elaine Haskell's house. "Can you make anything out of this?"

The flash in Owen's eyes was like sparks chipped from flint. "That's Elaine's handwriting. Where did you get this?"

"Never mind. What does it mean?"

"Elaine always left these cryptic notes laying around. There was no rhyme or reason to them. She did it vindictively, to drive everyone crazy."

"Did you doubt the authenticity of the letters?"

"At first, I did. We argued about it. Quite vehemently, in fact."

"Because you found them, and she took the credit?"

"Who told you that?"

"A little birdie. Do you know who Barber is?"

"I haven't the faintest idea."

"Who killed her, Owen?"

"The police felt they had the perpetrator in custody."

"Mark Keith? You know he didn't do it. The perpetrator is standing in front of me."

"Are you crazy?"

"No. But I'm right."

"If you're so convinced I killed Elaine, then why haven't the police locked me up?"

"I'm convinced. They aren't. And they won't believe me until I hand them some hard evidence that they had the wrong man."

"Are you that sure of yourself? Do you really know why people kill other people?"

"Sure. For love. For money. For personal gain. You stood to gain from Elaine Haskell's death, didn't you?"

"How?"

"New head of the Southport Historical Society, maybe? Chronicler of the Stanford Short letters?"

Before Harold Owen could reply, an icy voice spoke from the staircase landing. "Harold should have been named Executive Director of the Society before Elaine Haskell." A statuesque woman in a silk bathrobe regally descended the staircase, as though for her coronation. Moon recognized the exaggerated act that Owen had performed the day before at the Historical Society. The woman glided toward them, as if her feet were not in contact with the floor. The deep wrinkles in her aged face seemed like they'd been carved by a master's hand. Her eyes were a crystalline emerald green, and she wore her silver hair like a crown.

"Mrs. Owen?" Hazel Fine was right, thought Moon: Lydia Owen made an indelible impression.

"I find it odd that you would rouse us out of bed to impugn my son's character, Mr. Moon."

"You know me from somewhere?"

"I occasionally read your silly column in the tiresome local paper."

"It's all right, Mother," said Owen. His pugnacious attitude had suddenly become servile.

"Harold," she said in an off-hand, yet domineering tone. "Ask the gentleman to leave."

"Yes, Mother," he said, turning to Moon. "Answer one question. Do you have these missing letters—if there are any, that is?"

"No. But I know who does," Moon lied.

"If you do know who has them—which I doubt—they were stolen from the Historical Society."

"Says you."

"Good-bye, Mr. Moon," he said as he opened the door. A cold wind shook the chandelier—wind as cold as Mrs. Owen's stare.

"We're on different sides of the fence, Owen, you and me. You never had to put in an honest day's work in your life. You were given all of this"—Moon motioned to the interior of the home—"and you screwed up."

"That is a falsehood, Mr. Moon. And I detect a hint of envy in your voice. Had you had the chance, I doubt you would have done any better under identical circumstances."

"I sure as hell would like to have had that chance."

"Good-bye again, Mr. Moon," said Owen. His mother stood behind him, motionless as a statue.

"One more thing, Owen. Do you know a cop, a man by the name of Emmanuel Edison?"

"I've never heard the name. Why?" He licked his lips, while his eyes darted about.

"Don't insult my intelligence. You hired him to do your dirty work. He killed Elaine Haskell and Tessie Allen—at your command."

"That's outrageous! If you repeat this to anyone, I'll sue you. My lawyer is an expert in litigation."

"Just like a spoiled rich kid. Call the hired guns when trouble rides into town."

Owen slammed the door in Moon's face.

CHAPTER TWENTY-SIX
1865

The sun was high and hot when Short awoke the next day. The pain that pierced his head on all sides felt like rebel sabers. He smoothed down his rumpled uniform and went out in search of hot coffee. After he'd downed a few cups, he intended to pay a visit to Meriwether Pickens in the guard house. He thought he might be able to reason with Pickens about the letter. It was worth a try, anyway.

★★★

The sergeant in charge of the guardhouse was a tall, thick Irishman named Flynn who had no use for officers, so when he saw Captain Short coming down the footpath toward his post, he spit a thick stream of tobacco juice onto the ground and cursed under his breath. Bad enough he had to contend with the bunch of drunken Hoosiers that had come in the night before, now he had to deal with this pissant captain. He straightened and stood stiffly at attention, saluting the captain as he approached him.

"Sir!" he said.

Short returned the salute. "I'm here to inquire about a man I put on report yesterday, sergeant," said Short.

"Meriwether Pickens."

Flynn's eyes were puzzled as he raised his bushy, fire-engine red eyebrows. "No man by that name in here, sir. I'm sure of that."

Flynn gestured to the grassy area behind him. Like many wartime detention centers, the guardhouse was actually an open field, marked off and patrolled by sentries. There were nearly a hundred men in the field, most of them the drunken Hoosiers sleeping it off, but none of them Pickens.

"You're sure?" said Short.

"Sure as I am about anything, sir," said Flynn.

Short cursed and kicked at the ground. The corporal whom he had told to take Pickens to the guardhouse had obviously not done so, probably for a small bribe from the slimy Pickens. That meant that Pickens was lurking about somewhere.

"Son-of-a-bitch," Short said, pronouncing each syllable distinctly. "When I find that bastard, I'm going to have him bucked and gagged." A bucked and gagged soldier was made to sit on the ground, a stick was tied in his mouth and his hands tied together in front, knees thrust up between elbows. Another stick was then jammed between his arms and knees. The unfortunate would then have to sit in this unbearable position for the prescribed punishment time while other soldiers heaped abuse upon him.

"Bucked and gagged," said Short again, more to himself than the sergeant.

"Yes, sir," replied Flynn as Short stomped down the road. He would hate to be this Pickens fellow. The captain looked angry enough to have the man shot.

★★★

Short found Charlie Fay in front of his tent, sitting on a camp chair, cradling a cup of coffee in his hands. Fay's spacious wall tent, flaps up to let the balmy spring air through, was at the head of an orderly row of tents housing noncommissioned officers and enlisted men.

"Morning, Captain," said Fay with a smile. "Have some coffee."

Fay was of medium height and build, and his hair was the color of a rusty mower, but his most singular feature were his long, slender fingers—artist's fingers. Charlie's mother taught piano in Southport, and Charlie himself could play the instrument elegantly. When he sat and played the small piano in the parlor of the Short home in Southport, Stannie would watch his sister Elaine dreamily watching Charlie Fay. Short was sure that Fay felt the same affection for his sister, and he was happy for them. He would like nothing better than to have Charlie Fay as a member of his family. The two were as close as brothers anyway.

Short poured himself a cup of coffee from the pot sitting on the camp fire outside Fay's tent and then pulled up a camp chair next to Charlie's.

"It's going to be a grand review in Washington, I hear," said Charlie. "We're going to march in front of the President himself."

"Then home," said Short with a faraway voice.

"Home," said Fay, echoing his friend.

They sat in silence for a few moments, and then Short spoke: "Have you seen Meriwether Pickens around anywhere?"

"I have not had the displeasure," replied Fay. "Why?"

Short told him about the guardhouse incident, and Fay shook his head. "He's skulking about in the woods somewhere, no doubt," said Charlie. "Hoping you'll forget about what happened."

"Well, I won't," said Short. He wondered if he should tell Fay about the letter, but he finally decided against it. If it should ever come out in the open, he didn't want to suspect his best friend. He sipped the last of the coffee and set the cup on the ground. "I'm going to find that worthless skunk," he said as he stood and stretched.

"Good luck," said Charlie. "And be careful. Pickens would just as soon stick a knife in your ribs as look at you, Stannie. He hates you."

"The feeling is mutual."

As Short walked away, Fay returned to thinking about Short's sister, Elaine. He planned to write her a letter that evening, proposing marriage. He was sure she'd accept. Fay grinned and drank the last of his coffee.

CHAPTER TWENTY-SEVEN

1991

Moon stopped at DiCiccio's, stayed too long and drank too many whiskies in a vain effort to scrub the bad feelings from his soul after the visit with Owen and his iron-willed mama. Wealthy people made him nervous, and wealthy people who used their power and position to screw the system made him sick. Half a fifth of whisky did nothing to numb the feelings. Moon stupidly resisted Ralph's efforts to get him a cab and stumbled out to the Rambler, and miraculously managed to avoid any head-on collisions on the drive home. He flopped into bed fully-dressed and fell into a fitful sleep.

Moon's drunken dream unreeled in dark shadows like an old film noir: He was in the Historical Society; Tessie Allen lay on the floor in the archives. He heard her killer's footsteps rushing away and followed them into the pharmacy, into the ice cream shop, into the barbershop. There was the barber's chair, the mannequin-customer in turn-of-the-century clothes seated in the chair, the store-mannequin-barber's comb and scissors poised above his head. Neon blonde Elaine Haskell stood next to him, her hand on the barber's shoulder. A cryptic, teasing Mona Lisa smile split her face.

Moon sat bolt upright in the Murphy bed, its ancient

springs squeaking in protest. "Jesus!" he exclaimed. "That conniving bitch. That beautiful, brilliant, conniving bitch!"

Somebody in the next room hammered on the wall with his fist. The thin plasterboard trembled. "Shaddup!" a man hollered. "People are tryin' t' sleep!"

Moon dressed, hurrying out into the cold and snow.

★★★

When Moon reached the Queen Anne mansion, he walked around it and carefully checked the windows. He could make out the window bugs—strips of tape around the inside edges of each window, wired so that if the window were broken, an alarm would sound at the alarm system office, which would then call the police. He decided against shattering the glass and instead walked to the back door, which he figured was probably taped in the same fashion as the windows. On the door was a sign: "Caution! Premises Protected By Vanguard Alarm Systems!" Signs like this are meant to frighten burglars, but they don't.

There was also a four foot yellow police tape stretched across the door, signaling it to be a crime scene. Moon grabbed the tape with both hands and snapped it in two. Moon figured that the alarm system was pretty simple, like the one at the small northern-Wisconsin weekly he'd worked at before joining the *Southport Times*. Being the young, aggressive first-person-through-the-door-in-the-morning type at that time, he'd triggered the alarm more than once. A quick call to the alarm company usually stopped them from notifying the police and saved the paper's owners the twenty-five dollars in false-alarm charges. Crime scene or not, if they were called off, the cops wouldn't bother coming out here either. Moon knew the P.D. was stretched thin these days, due to budget cuts. The force was almost 50 cops short, and they were the most short-handed on the night-owl shift, where hard-pressed officers made most of the arrests.

It had better be a silent alarm, Moon thought. If a bell or a horn rang, he'd have to be out of there in a flash. In the interests of historic preservation, the Society had kept the mansion's original back door, trimmed in Victorian-style carpenter's lace. Not very secure in an age when doors were typically steel barriers to keep people out. In his haste, Moon had forgotten to bring a screwdriver to jimmy the door, but his worn wingtips had heavy leather soles. He memorized Vanguard's phone number on the sign, crossed his fingers and gave the flimsy wooden door a solid kick. It banged open and he raced inside, cut into the first doorway he found and grabbed a phone off someone's cluttered desk. He impatiently punched in the number he'd memorized.

"Vanguard Alarm," answered a feminine voice.

"Hello. This is Harold Owen at the Southport Historical Society. I'm afraid I accidentally tripped my alarm. I'm terribly sorry. I hope this isn't an inconvenience." Moon crossed his fingers and prayed she didn't know Owen's voice.

"Ok, Mr. Owen. Thank you for calling. We'll contact the police and let them know. What is your position at the Society?"

"I'm Assistant Executive Director."

"It's a little late to be there, isn't it? It's after one a.m."

"I'm doing some important research."

"Ok. We'll call the police. Thank you."

"Trusting soul," mumbled Moon. If she'd worked for him, he'd have fired her ass.

Moon wound his way up the back steps and down the long, gloomy hall past the exhibit rooms until he came to the barber shop. The scene was as in his dream: the barber perpetually poised to cut his customer's hair. A flick of the switch flooded the room with light. The barber wore a short white jacket, buttoned up to the collar. Moon patted down its front but felt nothing. He reached inside. Stuffed in the barber's pants, just a few inches below the waist, were several sheets of paper. He looked at the mannequin. Its red painted smile seemed to widen.

"Wipe that silly grin off your face," he said as he unbuttoned the pants. The old papers were in good condition, with a thick, cottony feel. Originals, not copies transcribed by Elaine Haskell. Moon zipped and buttoned the barber.

Moon walked to the archives, where no one had bothered to wash away the police outline of Tessie Allen's body. Moon stared at the stark white outline, and then flicked on the reading light screwed into the shelves.

The first sheet of paper was written in long, flowing script.

> Special Orders,
> HQ
> Guards and Patrols
> Will pass Stanford M. Short "Clerk" at these Hd. Qrs. at all hours, until further notice.
> By order of General Wm. T. Sherman
> Hd. Qrs. Dept. of the Army of the Tennessee
> City Point, Virginia
> March 27, 1865

The next sheet was a letter from Stanford Short, dated April 19, 1865, from Raleigh, North Carolina:

> Dearest Father,
> I write this letter to you in the utmost confidence. Things are not well here. General Sherman is greatly agitated over rumors that his peace terms with Rebel General Johnston are to the detriment of the union. We have had word of President Lincoln's assassination, and that perhaps an assassin will also make an attempt on General Sherman's life. Some of the soldiers here have

commented openly that the President should have been shot years ago. These traitors have been arrested. Others of the troop from Iowa have gone wild. They want to torch the town. Only the most persuasive arguments by their superior officers prevented a calamity such as happened in Columbia. You may have heard of the awful conflagration that recently consumed that Carolina city after our troops wreaked their vengeance upon it.

I assure you I was not a little surprised to hear that Freddy had enlisted and although I regret it very much, still I am glad 'tis for so short a season. The war is nearly over now, and it seems General Johnston will surrender his entire force over to us shortly. Freddy ought to have waited until my return anyway. One soldier at a time from our family is enough.
Affectionately, Stannie

The next letter was dated April 25, 1865, again from Raleigh:

Dearest Father,

I again urge you to remember your promise to me, should any of my letters contain disturbing battlefield news that you should keep them from Mother and my sister and brother.

It seems that Washington will not accept the surrender terms General Sherman has made with General Johnston, and that we again may have to go in the field to take arms against the southern armies. Would to God that every politician in the capital would be struck by lightning for the insanity of their decisions! General Sherman met with the rebel General in a modest log home near Durham Station here in North Carolina. The rebel General was ready, willing and able to surrender all of his forces on the spot and stop the bloodshed, yet General Grant has come here to tell General Sherman that he has given too lenient a peace to the southerners.

Too lenient a peace! As if one more dead Union soldier does

not make a difference, so long as the men in Washington can strut
and promenade for the fancy women of that corrupt and immoral
town. General Sherman is as low as I've ever seen him.
With Great Concern,
Stannie

Again, from Raleigh, dated April 28, 1865...

> Dearly Remembered Father,
> I have enclosed along with these letters a separate envelope,
> sealed. I wish you to store this envelope in a safe place until my
> return. Do not let anyone see it. It is for my private use only. I
> know you will respect my wishes, as I would respect yours. I will
> only tell you that this war is not yet over, and it may of yet take
> a dangerous and unexpected turn. I fear for the entire country if
> cooler heads do not prevail in this most trying of times. General
> Sherman is in such a state that I fear he may erupt at any
> moment. The Army is also in great consternation. Many soldiers
> openly talk of rebellion against Washington, and of teaching the
> politicians a lesson.
> I again remind you, dear father, to guard this envelope with
> your life.
> Stannie.

There was an envelope included with the letters. Its seal
had been broken. Moon pulled out a single sheet of paper
and read it. It was in a different hand, not Short's, and it was
difficult to decipher. Moon glanced at the clock on the wall.
It was 2:00 AM. He decided this was important enough to risk
Von Essen's wrath and moved to a phone to call him.

After seven rings, a sleepy, feminine voice answered,
"H'lo?"

"Is Karl in?"

"Who is this?"

"Tell him it's Moon. He's expecting my call."

"He is, huh? Well, I hope this ain't no crazy man." Moon heard her admonishing her husband as she handed him the phone.

"Yeah?" said Karl sleepily.

"It's me, Moon. I found the missing letters."

Von Essen's voice lost its grogginess, became animated. "Where?"

"Right here in the Historical Society. Will you look at them?"

"Of course! Bring them over now."

"Give me ten minutes."

Moon hurried to the copier in the archives, and made a copy of the letter in the envelope.

CHAPTER TWENTY-EIGHT

Moon detoured to his hotel on his way to Von Essen's, raced up the steps to his room and hid the letter in the envelope under some sweaters in his dresser drawer. He was no historian, but he knew that what he had seen was probably the cause of two murders, and he wasn't about to wave the original around and maybe cause another. His, for instance.

★★★

Avacado-colored nightgown wrapped tightly around her pear-shape, the woman who answered the door was a future Hippo-in-training. Her hair was a tangled mass of ebony wires, and there was a light dusting of black hairs above her lip. She stared at Moon with round brown eyes. "Are you the man who called on the phone?"

"Yes."

"You sure you ain't no crazy man?"

"No, I'm not sure." Her handshake was a soft, sensuous, electric charge. "I'm Moon."

"OK, Mr. Moon, come in. I'm makin' some coffee." Karl stood behind her, waving him in.

Moon watched Karl's wife walk into the kitchen, pendulous hips swaying rhythmically under her robe.

"I met Traci in Detroit a few years ago, when I was on a research project," said Karl, watching Moon watch his wife. "A government grant to trace the migration of blacks from the Old South to the industrial North. She was a different lady then. I first saw her on a beach, wearing a pink bikini the size of two Band-Aids, throwing a bright yellow beach ball in the air and laughing. I proposed to her two weeks later."

"I wish I could have been there to see it."

"It's amazing what eight years of marriage and two babies can do to the female figure," he sighed. "And disposition," he added. "But enough of my love life. What have you brought me?"

Moon handed him the original Short letters and the copy he had made.

"Oh," moaned Karl, reminding Moon of a guy in a floor-length raincoat in a porno movie house.

Von Essen opened the envelope. "My God," he muttered as he read. "Do you know what this is?" He shoved the copy toward Moon.

"Enlighten me, Karl."

"Look at the signature." He pointed to the bottom of the letter. *Wm. T. Sherman.*

Moon squinted. "I can't make it out."

"This letter was written by General William T. Sherman!" he said, his head bobbing joyously. "The tone and handwriting are his. But this is just a copy. Do you know where the original is? If we could get our hands on it—my God!"

"So what makes this letter so important?"

"It's dynamite. Pure, unadulterated nitro. It would knock historians on their collective fannies. For a Civil War historian, it would be the find of the century!"

Moon settled deeper into the sofa. "Read it to me," he said.

Von Essen began to read, hands trembling, pausing occasionally to decipher a word:

Raleigh, North Carolina, April 27, 1865
Edwin M. Stanton,
       Secretary of War
       Washington, D.C.

Stanton:
       The time for rumor and untruths is over. The recent newspa-
per articles, written by the seditious northern press that have only
just come to my attention prove this. You, Greeley, and the whole
of the rotten rabble in Washington and the press have proved
yourselves to be the traitors to the Cause, not me. My men have
died by the thousands because of the indiscretions of the press in
disclosing my troop strength and movements. I point to Greeley's
recent scurrilous recording of the movements of my force for all to
see, including the rebel General Hardee. And while these vile and
seditious traitors ply their nefarious trade, you call me traitor! The
time for idle talk is over and the time for aggressive action has
begun.
       Unless your resignation is on President Johnson's desk in three
days, I shall move my entire army to Washington, where I will
seize the government you now so ruthlessly control and hand it
back over to President Johnson to conduct the affairs of state
without your interference so that we may proceed with the final
surrender of the remaining rebel armies and reconstruction of the
southern states.
       Make no mistake about this. I have 100,000 battle-
hardened troops who will follow me to hell and back if I ask them
to. Grant and his army are miles away and I dare say he will not
oppose me as I believe he agrees with me on this matter. I stood by
Grant when he needed me, and he will stand by me now. Once I
sweep aside the defences around Washington, I will arrest both you

and Greeley and have you shot as traitors and spies. This war was
fought to preserve the Union and I can not stand idly by while you
foster disunion with your actions and your statements to the press.
Wm. T. Sherman

Von Essen's eyes were moist with emotion. "If you could
get the original of this, do you know what it would be worth?"

"More than a few bucks, huh?"

"In terms of historical scholarship, it's priceless."

"Translate that into dollars and cents for me."

"Who knows what an oil sheik or a Japanese businessman might drive the price up to? A million dollars, maybe?
People get weird around something like this."

"Why is it so valuable?"

"Anything with Sherman's signature is worth a lot of
money, even though he wrote voluminous correspondence.
But he was one of the pivotal figures during America's most
crucial period. What makes this letter unique is that it could
literally have changed the course of history."

"How?"

"Sherman hated the press, as I told you. He once threatened to have the reporters traveling with his army shot as
spies. He also hated Stanton, Lincoln's Secretary of War. Stanton
was a shrill, excitable character. For all intents and purposes,
Stanton ran the federal government after Lincoln's assassination. President Johnson was out of his league. Stanton hated
the South and he wanted to see it punished. Sherman gave
very lenient peace terms to General Johnston—this was after
Lee surrendered to Grant—and Stanton accused Sherman pub-
licly of being a traitor and intending to seize the government
and install himself as dictator. Every influential newspaper in
the north published his accusations verbatim."

"And this letter would prove that Sherman had just such
intentions?"

"Maybe not for the same reasons Stanton thought, but it would be proof positive that the thought had entered his mind. A letter like this could change entirely the historical perspective of Sherman. It certainly would be the subject of intense historical debate, at the very least."

He tapped the letters on his lap with an anxious finger. "And if we can find the original we could also prove that this boy, this Stanford Short, may have saved the country from a great catastrophe by stealing this letter. Think about it. Sherman moves on Washington. Grant moves to intercept. The north divides along lines of loyalty to the two generals. In the south, there are still a hundred and fifty thousand men at arms in the field. It boggles the mind."

"Could it really have happened?"

"Sherman was sometimes impetuous. He was undoubtedly under great stress and he may have written the letter, in part, to relieve that stress. But Stanton also may have gotten his hands on it, and therefore the northern press. The armies could have started moving of their own accord, like a snowball barreling down a hill, and nothing save a great battle would have resolved the issue. It could have been the Civil War all over again. Only this time, it would have been the boys in blue battling one another."

"Maybe this is a copy of a fake letter, Karl."

Karl shook his head. "No, this is the real thing. I'm sure of it. You've got to find the original."

"Do you really think it's worth a million dollars?"

"Like I said, some Japanese businessman or wealthy Arab could jack it up past that in an auction. It might bring in two million."

"That justifies two murders." Moon said as he took the letter from Karl. Von Essen released it reluctantly, fingertips caressing it for a few extra seconds.

"Now I've got to confront the man who killed Elaine

Haskell and Tessie Allen," said Moon. "I've got a favor to ask you."

"What?"

"Tell no one—no one—about these letters. Especially about the Sherman letter."

"I understand."

His wife entered the room with two cups of steaming hot coffee. "You're not staying for coffee?" she said as Moon zipped his parka.

"I can't, thank you. It was very nice meeting you."

"You are a crazy man." She shot an angry look at her husband, who winced and wilted under her stare.

CHAPTER TWENTY-NINE

Still shaky from his bout with the bourbon bottle at DiCiccio's, Moon pushed the Rambler through the snowbound streets, past the deserted American Auto Works. Shrouded in snow, the half-destroyed buildings resembled pictures he had seen of Richmond in the Civil War: ghostly sentinels whose empty windows were dead eyes filtering winter moonlight. A huge crane stood among the skeletal remains of the factory complex, silhouetted against the night sky like a giant praying mantis.

He wondered if the letter was indeed authentic—Von Essen obviously thought so, on the strength of only seeing a copy—and if it was, why a powerful man like Sherman would pen such an intemperate statement. But even with his limited knowledge of history, Moon knew the letter was an aberration—like a coin with a double-stamped die mark—one of those oddities that collectors put an enormous value on. But he wondered what value they'd put on the three lives that had been sacrificed—maybe more before the whole thing was over.

Moon didn't know yet if he would reveal the fact that he had the original Sherman letter. Something inside told him to keep it hidden away. He would have to work around the letter, using the Short letters to convince the police that Harold Owen, working with Manny Edison, was responsible for the deaths of Tessie Allen and Elaine Haskell. Convincing Southport's finest to arrest one of their own, however—no matter how odious—would be nearly impossible.

*** *** ***

It was nearing 3 a.m. when Moon pulled up in front of Sally's apartment complex. Two squad cars were parked at the curb, lights flashing. Moon approached a cop leaning against one of the squads—a pot-bellied man holding a paper cup of coffee in one hand, blowing against the cold in the other.

"You live here?" he asked Moon, nodding at the fake-Tudor building.

"No. A woman I know lives here," said Moon.

"Skinny broad? Nice looking? Black hair?"

"Don't say 'broad,'" Moon chided. "What's the problem?"

"They took her outta here about fifteen minutes ago to City Hospital. Somebody busted into her apartment and beat her up real good."

*** *** ***

There's nothing more desolate than the inside of a hospital at three in the morning. You can feel the disease and the pain flowing through the deserted halls.

The solitary receptionist at the front desk of massive City Hospital was a short, pencil-thin woman with garish hair and high cheek bones that gave her an Oriental appearance. In an efficient and slightly prissy manner, she thumbed quickly through her charts to answer Moon's question about Sally's room number. "Andrews? It's three-oh-eight. But visiting hours are over," she protested as Moon hurried away, his long winter coat trailing behind him like a cape. Batman, he thought, taking the steps three at a time. Captain America. Some hero.

Sally's bed was raised at an almost forty-five degree angle. Her eyes were closed, and her right arm was in a sling. Moon couldn't see any bruises. Outside of the sling, she seemed no worse for the wear.

"What's up, punkin?" he said as he approached her bed. Then he saw the vicious bruise on her right arm.

She opened one eye slowly. "Oh, Moon," she moaned, her voice cracking in pain.

Moon felt rage and hate surge through him as though it were he who had been violated. He reached out and touched the bruise lightly. "So what happened?" he said soothingly. "I heard tales of death and destruction when I pulled up in front of your apartment."

"Oh, jeez. It was that awful man."

"Owen?"

"No. That policeman who came to my apartment the other day. The one who hates you so much."

"Manny Edison?"

"Yes. I was sleeping, and he started banging on my door. I didn't see any reason not to let him in. He barged past me with this big pistol in his hand. He looked like 'Dirty Harry.'"

"What happened?"

"He demanded to know where you were, and I told him I didn't know."

"You weren't lying. Then what?"

"He said he didn't believe me, and he started to search the apartment. I told him you weren't there. Then he asked for the letters. I told him I didn't know anything about any letters, and then he said, 'You know what letters, you bitch!'"

"He called you that?"

"He sure did. I saw red and slapped his face. It stunned him for a moment, but then he came at me with the pistol. I held up my arm to protect myself, and the gun caught my arm. It hurt, because he hit the bone, and I thought for a minute he'd broken my arm."

"What happened then?"

"He said, 'Who is Mr. Barber?'"

"What did you say?"

"I said, 'How the hell would I know who Mr. Barber is?'"

"And then?"

"Then he said 'You tell your boyfriend I know who Mr. Barber is, and he better stay away from him.'"

"He's a day late and a dollar short. What did he do then?"

"He tried to hit me again, this time on the face. But I fell and covered my face with my arms. He ran out, fast as he came in. I'd be careful, Moon. He's looking for you, and the letters."

"I've got them right here, compliments of Mr. Barber." Moon patted his coat pocket. "And they're dynamite."

"Are you going to let me read them?"

"Later. Right now, I think you should rest."

"I am, Moon. They gave me some pain killers. I'm all doped up. I'm going to lie back and sleep straight through the night. I'm going home tomorrow."

"We'll see what the doctor says about that."

"Will you call work for me and tell them I won't be in?"

"OK. I've got to go now. You rest, and I'll be back later."

"Moon ..."

"What?"

"I know what you're thinking. You're going to go after Edison. I told you that Mark Keith and Tessie Allen weren't your responsibility. Neither am I. Whatever happened to me tonight is my problem, not yours."

"Don't worry about me. I can take care of myself."

"This is no film noir, Moon. This is the real thing." She closed her eyes. "And for God's sake, don't have a testosterone attack, Godzilla. You could get more than your lights punched out this time."

She was right, he thought. It wasn't his business. It never had been. He had stuck his nose in where it didn't belong, playing a child's game and had endangered this good, gentle woman in the process. But he was going to put an end to this nonsense. Tonight.

"No, Sally," he said as she drifted off to sleep. "Not this time."

CHAPTER THIRTY

Moon knew where he'd find Manny Edison.

He parked the Rambler in front of the Historical Society, behind Edison's sleek black sports car and a late-model Lincoln. The entire second floor of the building was lit up like a Christmas tree. Harold Owen, Moon thought. Good. He'd kill two birds with one stone—or, in this case, bat.

Moon played right field for "The Hometown Heroes," DiCiccio's sixteen-inch softball team every summer and carried his equipment in his car year 'round. He opened the trunk and pulled out a softball bat, grabbed the taped handle with both hands and viciously sliced it through the frigid air. As he started to walk resolutely toward the building, Manny Edison suddenly materialized out of the gloom, not ten yards from him.

"I'm gonna kill you, Manny," Moon said behind clenched teeth.

"Strictly bush league, Mr. Writer." Manny's grin was a razor-thin slash as he watched Moon heft the baseball bat into a defensive position. A powdery dusting of snow covered Manny's leather coat and baseball cap. He took a threatening step forward, lifted his hand, and leveled his pistol at Moon.

"Bye, bye," he said.

Fire and thunder leaped from the barrel of Manny's .44 as Moon hit the sidewalk, briefly knocking himself senseless. He lay there for what he thought was half a minute, got up slowly, grunting and feeling for where the bullet had hit him. Miraculously, Manny had missed—probably thinking he'd hit him when he slammed into the sidewalk. Moon retrieved his bat and followed Manny's footprints in the snow to the back door of the building. He heard the thump of a pistol shot, followed by the crack of a second shot.

Moon caught his breath. Good God. Manny Edison must have just dusted Harold Owen!

The back door was just as Moon had left it: kicked in, flapping in the winter wind. He wound his way up the back stairs to the second floor, through the archives and into the brightly lit hallway housing the period rooms. As he expected, he could hear frantic rummaging in the Barber Shop. It looked like Edison hadn't been bluffing at Sally's. He had figured out who Mr. Barber was. Moon hoisted the bat onto his shoulder. He wasn't going to give the cop a second chance at him. Give Edison a nanosecond to react, and he'd blow a hole in Moon just like he'd done to so many others. The first thing Edison was going to get from Moon was the bat on the back of his rotten little skull.

Moon crept silently down the hall. When he reached the barber shop he raised the bat to crack Manny Edison's head and got the shock of his life: Harold Owen was crouched over the tipped-over barber chair, his hands stuffed up the pants leg of the customer-dummy. He was cursing nonstop— so creatively foul that he would have stunned a dock workers' convention. Crumpled in one corner of the small room was the lifeless body of Manny Edison, his .44 held clutched in his outstretched hand.

"Tsk, tsk," Moon said loudly. "Such language. Is this how

historians get their jollies, fondling store dummies? If that's your bag, you should buy one of the blow-up kind. They're much softer, feel like the real thing."

Owen looked up, startled, like a deer caught in headlights. "You sonofabitch!"

"Beat you to it, didn't I? Mr. Barber has already coughed up his secrets to me." Moon patted his coat pocket, feeling the reassuring bulge of the letters. "It was quite a surprise finding you here. When I heard the shots, I was expecting to find him alive," Moon gestured with the bat to Manny's life-less corpse, "and *you* dead."

Owen plunged his hand in his coat pocket and pulled out a small silver-barreled pistol and leveled it at Moon's chest. "He was a traitor," Owen yelled hysterically. "I hired him to find the Sherman letter, and he was going to keep it for him-self. He tried to kill me, but I shot him first." He stared at the cop's body. Moon hadn't noticed the neat little hole just be-low Edison's left eye. Manny's nose wouldn't be telling him anything anymore.

"Give me those letters," said Owen. "I found them. They're mine."

"I found them," said Moon. "Doesn't that make them mine?"

Owen's glasses slipped down the bridge of his nose as he stepped closer toward Moon. Sweat beaded on his eyebrows. "Where is the Sherman letter?" he demanded.

"You mean this?" Moon pulled out the copy he'd made a few hours earlier. Owen snatched it greedily.

"This is a copy!" he said. "Where's the original?"

"That's what I found with the Stanford Short letters," Moon lied. "I'm not up on my history. Is it significant?"

"A copy has no significance. Did you make this copy? The public has a right to know about this letter. And you have no right to keep it from them."

"I didn't copy anything." Moon put on his best poker face, the one he'd learned playing penny-ante five-card stud with his mother in their kitchen. She used to laugh, watching Moon try to put on a dead-pan face like a grown-up playing for real money.

Owen stomped his foot like a little boy who demands a toy forbidden to him. "Then it was Elaine. She must have made the copy and hid the original. I found the letters first, and Elaine took them from me. She was going to take all the credit."

"So you had Manny whack her on the head with a hammer, and drag her out in the snow to freeze to death. Then you let an innocent man take the fall, and he hanged himself in jail. But I guess in the interests of scholarship, all that's justified."

"No!" he said, shaking his head violently, his glasses flying off his face. "I didn't do that. I was angry enough to order her assassination, but I didn't."

"Tessie Allen?"

He motioned to the corpse in the corner. "His handiwork."

"And it was Manny who conked me on the head in the basement and shot at me outside Haskell's house?"

The little man smirked. "I was the one outside Elaine's house that night. I was trying to get in, to find the Sherman letter. I only shot at you to frighten you away. You were becoming a real pest."

"My friends tell me the same thing. I should have figured it wasn't Manny. He wouldn't have tried to ambush me. He would've stood on the back porch and blasted me off the steps when I came out of the house."

Owen retrieved his glasses from the floor, keeping the pistol leveled at Moon's chest, and put them back on his face. One of the lenses had splintered, hairline cracks radiating from the center like a spider's web to the thick black frame. "Elaine

Haskell was ruthless. When I discovered the Stanford Short letters, and the Sherman letter, she claimed them for herself. I told her that we had to authenticate them before we released them for publication, but she would have none of that. She said that *she* was enough authority to assert their authenticity and that she was going to release them immediately. Her career couldn't wait for others to authenticate them, she said. I searched her office for the letters, but she had hidden them. Then I hired detective Edison to assist me, but just when it seemed we had the Sherman letter in our grasp, he turned on me."

"Right in character for Manny."

"A few hours after you left my home this evening, I deduced what Elaine had meant by 'Barber.' I told Edison, and he went to your girl friend's apartment to question you. I came here and saw the back door kicked open."

"And you brought your pistol with you?"

"I began to have doubts about my hireling." Blood trickled out of the hole below Manny Edison's eye.

"Good call—one that probably saved your life."

"Not yours, however. Now I have to kill you, too. Like him." Owen glanced at Manny's body, and Moon quickly swung the bat at him, connecting with his head with a loud clunk. Owen sank to the floor in a disheveled heap. Moon bent and took the pistol from his limp hand.

"We're going to have to go visit the police, you know," said Moon.

Owen groaned as he sat and looked up at Moon. "You're going to have to make me."

"I have the gun."

Owen sneered. "You hate me, don't you?"

"You're right. I hate tight-ass rich kids who had everything handed to them on a platter."

"And who are you, conscience for the world's disadvan-

taged? I heard enough pontificating from your ilk in the Sixties, and when push came to shove, you copped out for the
secure middle-class lifestyle you were protesting against. Your
act is pathetic, you know that?"

The words were on target, and they stung Moon more
than he'd ever admit. Moon offered Owen a hand. "Come on,
Owen. Let's go." He pulled the scholar up.

"Mother will never forgive me," Owen moaned.

In the corner, Manny Edison lay shriveled in his crumpled
leather coat, which covered him like a worn, discarded snake
skin.

CHAPTER THIRTY-ONE

Detective Tony O'Connor had a classic cop's face—world-weary, tinged with profound sadness. Charged with the Elaine Haskell/Tessie Allen investigations, he'd been ready to wrap up an exhausting week and go home to a hot supper, a couple of hours with his wife and kids and twelve hours of sleep. But a half hour before his shift ended there had been a call about a fight at a party, where some idiot neighbor, pissed off by the noise next door, had barged out of his house and threatened three teenagers with an axe handle. The jerk hadn't been aware of the first rule of brawling: If you pull a weapon, you better be prepared to use it. He wasn't. The kids had taken the axe handle, beat the shit out of him and then one of them had plunged a buck knife into his chest. The unfortunate guy died in a pool of blood. The kids were in custody, one of them the son of a County Board member who had spent two hours haranguing the detective to release his kid on a signature bond. The County Board member had exited in a huff; his kid was still in the lock-up, and Tony O'Connor looked thoroughly pissed off and desperately in need of sleep as Moon dragged Harold Owen through his office door.

"What the hell is this, Moon?" The detective reached for

his coffee, but the incensed County Board member had put out his cigarette in the cup and the butt floated unappetizingly in the cold, inky fluid. O'Connor made a sour face and tossed the coffee into his waste basket.

"This is the guy that probably had Elaine Haskell killed," said Moon.

Owen lunged at him, fists clenched, but the detective grabbed him in midair. "I did not!" Owen screamed.

"He's got the motive Tony. Check it out."

"This guy? A murderer? What evidence do you have?"

"This, Tony." Moon tossed the Stanford Short letters on his desk.

The cop casually fingered them. "What is this crap?" he grunted.

Owen jabbed a finger at Moon. "Ask him about the Sherman letter."

"What's he mean?" Tony tried to sound interested, but he was wondering whether his wife was keeping his dinner hot. Pot roast and homemade noodles—his favorite meal—and these two bozos were keeping him from it.

"I don't know, Tony. I think he's hallucinating. First, he accuses me of lying. Now he says I've got this ...what was it again?"

Owen eyed him angrily from behind his thick glasses. "The Sherman letter!" he screamed. "You know what I mean!"

He began to bounce on the balls of his feet. Moon wondered if he pulled the same stunt on his parents when he was a little boy. Tony O'Connor grabbed him by the shoulders to slow him down. "Take it easy, sport."

"There's a few other things, Tony," said Moon.

"Like what?"

"Like Manny Edison is lying in a corner at the Historical Society. Dead." Moon tossed Owen's pistol on the cop's desk. "Owen shot him with this."

The detective stared at Owen, incredulous. "You took out Manny Edison?"

Moon chuckled. "Ain't that the cat's ass?"

"He tried to shoot me first," whined Owen.

"I don't doubt that," said Tony. "But you? You wasted the Son of Sam?"

"And Mr. Owen here also claims that Manny Edison killed the old lady—Tessie Allen."

"He did," said Owen. "He was endeavoring to get her to reveal where the Sherman letter was hidden. He shoved her, and she struck her head on the bookshelves. He confessed to me that he did it."

"That Sherman letter again," said the cop. "Can you produce this letter?"

"No," said the historian. "Not the original anyway."

The cop tossed the letters in the air. They fluttered to the floor like paper wings. "More crap! This thing has gotten out of hand, Moon," he said. "I've had nothing but grief since Haskell was killed. Now the Chief, with a lot of coaxing from your old lady at Social Services, has decided we need sensitivity training, because of that kid hanging himself in his cell. What a joke!"

"My *ex* old lady," Moon replied, reminding the detective that he and Marsha had cut the knot. "Do you need a statement from me or something?"

"Yes, I do," said the detective. "If you'll spare me an hour or two."

"Sensitivity training, my ass," Tony mumbled sarcastically as Moon left for the interrogation room.

"So you've found your killer, have you?" said Hippo, forcing a weak smile. Moon had to grudgingly admit that there were too many loose ends in the hopeless tangle he'd voluntarily

mired himself in. Those loose ends forced him to search out
the bookie and see if he might provide any answers. Finding
him was an easy task. He would be eating his way through
Southport, using his free time to add to his already impressive bulk. Moon knew he had the habit of taking early breakfast at a Ramada Inn situated on the lake.

"Correction: I've found one killer. I need to find another."
Moon eyed Hippo's plate. "Cheeseburgers for breakfast?"

Hippo dumped ketchup and mustard on two thick cheeseburgers with focused concentration. Ten white tablecloths away
in a far corner of the room, Dean Paskewicz idly leafed through
the Milwaukee Sentinel sports wrap.

The Ramada Inn's wide bank of windows looked out over
the port. Beyond them, the sun was a blazing yellow ball
about a foot off the horizon. Two snow-encrusted piers de-
fining the harbor stretched out to the east, the skinny red
lighthouse on the north pier flashing its light. Vapor rose from
the icy waters. A flock of gulls floated on a large sheet of ice
in the middle of harbor, beaks buried in their breasts against
the cold.

"A cheeseburger is an all-around meal, my friend," said
Hippo. "You've got your meat, your bread, your greens." He
put a slice of onion, tomato, and a bit of lettuce on top of the
meat, placed the top of the bun over the whole works and bit
it like a snapping turtle deftly cutting a hapless bug in two.
He chewed in silence as he scrutinized Moon. Moon raised a
hand to his face, to shield his eyes from the piercing dawn
sun as well as from Hippo's relentless stare.

After Moon related the past night's events, Hippo asked:
"Isn't it possible that Manny Edison could have murdered
Elaine Haskell as well?"

Moon shook his head in denial. "No, it wasn't his style.
He would have plugged her with that oversized pistol or beat
her into a bloody pulp, and he wouldn't have cared much

who would have suspected him. He's been getting away with so much for so long that he felt he was above the law."

"I agree. Elaine's murder was done much too neatly." Hippo swallowed the last of the cheeseburger with a great gulp and washed it down with orange juice. Moon licked his lips, bone dry from last night's whiskey.

Hippo patted his fat lips with a napkin. He gestured to a small piano bar tucked away in a corner of the large dining room. The bar was closed, but a wide-screen television was tuned to CNN and live coverage of the Gulf War. Two waitresses and the hostess were leaning against the bar, watching the screen intently. One waitress bit her fingernails nervously.

"The great battles of this war won't be fought in the sands or the skies of Arabia," Hippo sermonized, nodding toward the anxious women transfixed by the television. "It's going to be fought there"—he pointed to the TV with a thick finger— "on the television screen. Mark my words."

"It ought to fuel the debate about war versus the press. I'll bet everyone's going to accuse us of aiding and abetting the enemy."

"Us?" replied Hippo. "I'm shocked you'd lump print journalists with their broadcast brethren. Television is too quick to judge. It doesn't leave enough time for reflection."

"General Sherman hated the press during the Civil War. He accused us of being the enemy."

"You've learned a bit about history in pursuit of your murderer, haven't you, Moon?"

Hippo noticed Moon's disappointment. "You were positive it was Harold Owen who killed Elaine, weren't you?"

"Yes, I was. But now I know it wasn't. That's why I need help." Hippo shook his head gravely. "You know something I don't?" Moon asked.

"Perhaps. I'd call your pursuit a shotgun approach to the problem."

"What else am I going to do?"

"I could give you a list of names. You could proceed down that list, checking and cross-checking until you've satisfied yourself that your killer is or is not on the list. But not what I'd call very efficient."

"What do you suggest?"

"Going back to square one."

"Which is?"

"Owen. He had the motive and access to Elaine Haskell. You already know who murdered Tessie Allen."

"He vehemently denies having anything to do with Elaine Haskell's murder, Hippo. I *wanted* him to be the guilty party, but now, I can't imagine Owen sneaking into her home and murdering her while she was passed out on her couch. You know, I had concentrated so hard on getting that guy ..."

"We all make mistakes."

"So where does that leave me?"

"As much as you may hate to admit it, you're a bulldog, Moon. An excellent newsman. Act like one."

Peeved, Moon asked, "And how does an excellent newsman act?"

"You pursue the story to its logical conclusion."

"Which is?"

Hippo sighed impatiently, rolling his eyes. "In my opinion, Harold Owen wouldn't have killed Elaine Haskell. He doesn't have the guts. But *another* Owen might well have done it."

CHAPTER THIRTY-TWO

1865

Stanford Short could barely conceal his rage. The thought that Meriwether Pickens had bribed the corporal into allowing him to escape punishment infuriated the captain.

"Bucked and gagged," Short repeated to himself over and over. He crashed through the woods encircling the enormous camp. He'd find Pickens if it took him all day and night.

★★★

Pickens hid in a rock outcropping close to the picket line. Even though the peace treaty with Johnston had been signed three days earlier, there were still vestiges of rebel activity in the area, as disgruntled soldiers continued to harass the Union camp. Pickens had it all figured out. He knew that Short would come looking for him, once he found out he hadn't been put in the guard house, and that Short would search through the woods for him if he couldn't be found in camp. When Short showed his face, it would be a simple matter of a quick aim-and-shoot.

Pickens caressed the old Sharps carbine he had stolen from someone's tent earlier in the day, ran his hand down the heavy barrel and the worn stock. If he hit Short dead center with this, he thought, he would tear a hole in his back big enough to drive a team and wagon through. His chuckle displayed yellowing teeth as he balanced the musket on a rock and sighted down the clearing in the woods where he was sure Short would appear at any moment.

"C'mon, you bastard," he hissed. "C'mon!"

✯✯✯

Short had worked up quite a sweat beating the bushes for Pickens. He looked up and saw by the position of the sun that it was nearly noon. His stomach told him the same thing, and he decided he'd break for lunch just after he searched one more section of woods. He stepped through a break in the trees and into a small clearing. At one end, maybe fifty yards away, there was an outcropping of rock. A good hiding place, thought Short as he walked toward it.

✯✯✯

Short appeared through the break in the trees, just as Pickens had expected. Better than that, as he walked toward the rocks, his chest loomed like a huge blue target. Pickens couldn't believe his good luck. He pulled back the hammer of the Sharps and leveled it at Short's chest. He let him come closer. Fourty yards ... thirty ...twenty ...

"Take this, you little peckerwood!" he shouted as he pulled the trigger. The rifle kicked and roared, and Short fell instantly, a hole big enough to stick a thumb into erupting in his chest. Clutching the rifle, Pickens emerged from behind the rocks and cupped a hand to the side of his mouth. "Sniper!" he yelled. "Reb sniper!"

Pickens heard the confused shout of the pickets as they moved toward the sound of his voice.

He disappeared from the woods and ran down the road back toward camp.

CHAPTER THIRTY-THREE

1991

The imposing residences lining the elegant street were dwarfed by the four-story Owen home—its snow-hooded roof like the white-haired head of an ancient soldier, its windows reflecting the sun like eyes glazed from incessant warfare.

Me, too, thought Moon. In the last few days, I've fought too many battles, seen too many deaths.

Lydia Owen answered the door on the first ring. She was wrapped tightly in the same robe she had worn the night before—like a caterpillar in its cocoon, bracing for the inevitable day when it would spread its wings and show its true colors.

"Harold is in trouble," she said matter-of-factly.

"You could safely say that," replied Moon. "May I come in?"

"I knew something was wrong when he didn't come home last night. Where is he?"

"He's downtown in the city lockup, actually. He shot a cop. Man by the name of Emmanuel Edison." She swayed, put out a hand, and steadied herself by clutching the door jamb. Moon reached out and grabbed her arm, surprised to feel soft, pliable flesh. She was human after all.

"I'm all right, thank you," she said icily, shaking his hand off her arm as if he had violated her.

"May I come in, Mrs. Owen?" he asked again. "You must be cold. I know I am."

"Come in, then," she said, standing aside to allow him into the foyer. "Would you like a cup of coffee?"

"That would be nice, thank you."

"Come into the living room." Moon followed her into a ballroom-sized room, with a large fireplace at the far end and thick cherrywood beams on the ceiling. Moon took a seat on the sofa closest to the doorway and examined the room. It was stuffed with French provincial furniture, much of it covered with a colorful peacock print. Oriental rugs, all of them antique and some of them threadbare, he thought, were scattered on the polished oak floor. Any one of them was worth more than he made in a year. On the walls—besides half a dozen large oil paintings by artists unknown to Moon—were dozens of photos of Harold Owen: Harold as a little boy on his tricycle; Harold with Santa next to a giant Christmas tree; Harold at about age 18 in a tux, holding hands with a not-very-pretty girl in a prom formal with a large corsage pinned at her breast. Then Harold in a graduation gown; as a young man, standing outside a college dorm; and in his office at the Southport Historical Society. In every photo, Harold looked uncomfortable, as if he wished he were somewhere else and not in the crosshairs of the camera's lens.

Lydia Owen strode into the room and handed Moon an ironstone mug. "Your coffee, Mr. Moon." The steaming cup was too hot to handle comfortably, so he set it on the coffee table. "Tell me exactly what happened to Harold," she said.

Lydia Owen sat opposite Moon like she was strapped in an electric chair: straight-backed and stiff as a board, hands tightly gripping the arms. Moon wondered if she had the ability to relax anywhere, ever. He told her about how he had found her son rummaging in the Historical Society, looking for the lost Short letters, with Manny Edison lying dead in a corner; how he had taken him to the police station, where he would also probably be booked for the murder of Elaine Haskell.

When he had finished the story she sighed and shook her head sadly. "Poor Harold," she said. "Poor, poor Harold." There was no sympathy in her analytical complaint.

"He's in quite a bind, Mrs. Owen. He's going to need your help."

"I don't know if I'm going to give it to him. I'm tired of saving that boy from himself."

Moon stared at her in disbelief. "This is your son we're talking about, lady. He's going to be booked for Murder One. In all probability, he'll be accused of a second. Do you know what'll happen to him if he's sent to prison? Men behind bars are not very refined."

Her countenance was pure granite. "I don't think he'll mind."

"You mean he likes boys?"

"Harold doesn't like boys," she replied dryly. "Nor does he like girls."

"You mean he's asexual?"

"That is the clinical term for my son's condition." Her casual glance swept the photos on the walls. "Sullivan and I so wanted a grandson," she said. "To carry on the family line."

"And Harold didn't oblige you. I guess that's as good a reason as any to let him fry for murder."

"My son has always been a disappointment to me. And to my husband. We had planned a great career in industry for him. All he had to do was ask for it. When he decided to pursue this ridiculous history career, we almost disowned him. I think he had a lot to do with my husband's heart attack. It

killed him, you know." Her eyes locked on another photo on
the wall, of a man in a 1930s pin-striped business suit. He
had an oval, self-satisfied, pasty face. Round spectacles were
balanced on the bridge of his nose, and his striped tie was
held by a diamond stickpin. It was an anonymous face, but
something beyond that came through. Moon imagined a pencil moustache, a black uniform, and a peaked military cap:
He was a dead ringer for one of those bland Nazis who hung
around Hitler, anxious to do his ghoulish bidding.

"My husband was a good man," insisted Lydia Owen, as
if she were reading his thoughts.

"I'm sure he was, Mrs. Owen. You aren't seriously con-
sidering leaving your son to the mercy of the legal system,
are you?"

"I am. He's never done anything correctly in his life."

"Like when he found the Stanford Short letters and let
Elaine Haskell buffalo him out of them?"

"That was a travesty," she said sternly.

"And when Elaine Haskell was given the Executive Directorship of the Society?"

"She was promoted over Harold. He had been there many
years before her, and the board passed over him."

"Shoddy treatment for the son of one of the wealthiest
and most influential families in Southport."

Lydia squinted her eyes suspiciously.

Moon watched her over the rim of his steaming coffee.
"You do agree, don't you? Your son's treatment was an insult
on the whole family—to you, in particular."

"We have had a certain position in the community, one of
responsibility and leadership."

'And now your son has sullied that position."

Lydia's reply was to sit even more stiffly, to try to stare
him down, a technique that must have been very effective
with Harold over the years. Moon suddenly felt very sorry for

the sad little boy in the photos on the wall. How hard it must have been for him to live up to his parents' expectations.

"Are you going to leave your son's butt hanging in the breeze? Is he going to take the fall for Elaine Haskell's' murder?"

"You said yourself that Harold denies killing Elaine."

"But the police will undoubtedly try to connect him with her murder. They're very good at doing that, you know. And they'll be doubly vigilant with your son, because they jailed an innocent man who then committed suicide in his cell. And don't forget the cop he shot dead last night. No, it doesn't look good for Harold. Unless ..."

"Unless what?" She was twitching slightly, as if the chair had become suddenly uncomfortable.

"Unless we tell them what really happened that night at Elaine Haskell's house."

"What do you mean?"

"You know, don't you?"

"No, I don't. Do *you* know what happened?"

"I can make a calculated guess—if you'd like me to, that is."

"Please do. I'm curious to hear your theory."

"OK." Moon leaned forward, elbows on his knees, coffee cup between his palms. "You killed Elaine Haskell."

Lydia arched one eyebrow, the most animated move he had seen her make. "Interesting," she replied matter-of-factly. "Continue."

"You were waiting for her that night when Mark Keith— the cabbie—brought her home. You were hiding somewhere. You probably saw the scene Mark described to me, when Elaine Haskell stripped and made a pass at the cabbie. When he left, she was lying there on the sofa, out cold. You sneaked out of your hiding place, carefully lifted her hair and whacked her behind the ear with a ball-peen hammer—which is probably hidden somewhere here in your house. It took all your strength, but you hit her as hard as you could, a single blow. You put her hair back in place—and this is the part that really gets me—you dressed her before dragging her outside to freeze in the snow. You must be a pretty strong lady, for your age. Just how old are you?"

"I'm ten years younger than Tessie Allen was," she said in an oddly triumphant tone.

Moon did some quick figuring in his head. "Seventy," he said. "Well, stranger things have happened. The hammer blow didn't kill her, you know. She froze to death. Pretty cruel way to die, don't you think?"

"How did you form this outrageous hypothesis?" she asked casually. But Moon noticed her hands had gripped the chair's arms more tightly.

"I got some help, actually. From a slothful but brilliant man who eats cheeseburgers for breakfast. The rest I just played by ear—right now, while we've been talking."

"Impressive," she said. "But how do you plan to go about proving your story?"

"Good question. The hammer, for one thing, must have some bits of hair, bone or blood on it that will match Elaine Haskell's blood type and the size of the wound. She's been buried already, so we'll have to get an exhumation order. The cops have swept her house. If they have any hairs or fibers that match you or your clothing, it will put us one step closer toward indicting and convicting you."

"Do you seriously think you can get a court order to exhume Elaine Haskell's body, if I stand in your way? Do you think the police will follow your preposterous theory, once they find out it's directed against me?"

"I do, Mrs. Owen. This is nineteen ninety-one, not nineteen thirty-nine. The Owen name doesn't carry as much weight as it used to."

"If you pursue this any further, beyond this room, you'll be hearing from my attorneys." She looked to her husband's photo on the wall, as if for strength in her crisis.

"That will be fine," Moon said as he pulled a business card out of his wallet and threw it onto the coffee table. "Here's my attorney's card. Have your lawyers contact him."

She gazed at him in astonishment. "You're not serious?"

"I am. I may be a lot of things, Mrs. Owen, but in a situation like this, I feel I have the moral high ground—and I'm going to keep it."

Still in open-mouthed astonishment, she said, "I don't believe I'm hearing this. In this day and age ..."

"Now I have a confession to make, Mrs. Owen," Moon interrupted. "I confess that sometimes—most of the time—I'm too quick to judge. I set my standards too high and no one, least of all me, can live up to them. It's one of the reasons my wife left me. Your son had me pegged on that point. He knew I judged him as a rich spoiled kid because he had all the things I never had. It's hard for me to admit, but it's true." He exhaled, feeling like a marathon runner the day after the big race, when his body tells him it needs a long, uncomplicated rest.

"Besides," he continued, "I've been up all night, most of the past five nights. I'm dead-tired. I've been shot at and hit over the head. A good woman was attacked by a rip-off cop, and she's in the hospital. Tessie Allen, an old lady who wouldn't have harmed a fly, has been cruelly murdered. You let an innocent man take the rap for your crime, and he killed himself in despair."

"A cab driver," she interrupted, dismissing Mark Keith with a casual wave. "A man of no consequence."

"Maybe so. But an innocent man of no consequence. That pisses me off. All of it pisses me off. And last of all, I don't like the way you're throwing your boy to the wolves."

He abandoned her to her chair, so brittle that he feared she would crack into a million pieces.

CHAPTER THIRTY-FOUR
1865

Watching his friend stomp away in search of Pickens, Charlie
Fay thought back to the concert the evening before. A regi-
mental band from Wisconsin had stood on the grounds before the grand house the General used as his headquarters
and sang a new song about the now world-famous March to
the Sea. The singer, a fine Irish tenor, was backed up by a
competent ensemble of brass (not cheap tin) instruments.
Sherman had strolled out onto the porch and smiled, calmly
puffing on his cigar as the band serenaded him.

The singer sang:

"Our campfires shone bright on the mountain,
"That frowned on the river below,
"While we stood by our guns in the morning,
"And eagerly watched for the foe.

"Then a horseman rode out from the darkness,
"That hung over mountain and tree,
"And shouted 'Boys up and be ready!
"For Sherman will march to the sea."

Charlie stood next to Stannie and let the music carry him back to the very beginning. The hard training at Camp Henry, the spirited march through Southport, the column led by Colonel Daniels on a "Fine, spirited black horse, fully caparisoned," as stated in the local papers. And then the many battles. The cavalry skirmish in the fight at Cape Girardeau, Missouri, where he had seen an artillery shell take off a Confederate cavalryman's head, the head falling one way off the horse, the body, the other, like a flower snapped off its stem. The fierce engagement at Chalk Bluff, where he thought he had bought it, a Minie ball tugging at his shoulder, passing through his shirt without leaving a scratch, but the force of it strong enough to knock him off balance and off his horse. Chickamauga, where both Union and Confederate generals died like flies and enlisted men died even faster. He could taste the acrid smoke in his mouth, feel it sting his eyes, heard the anguished cries of the thousands, blue and gray, cut down in battle. And under a fierce Confederate onslaught, the withdrawal to Chattanooga.

Three days later, they attacked a column of Joe Wheeler's dismounted cavalry plundering a Union supply train. The Union cavalry's successive saber charges pushed the Confederates back again and again. It was at this engagement that Colonel LaGrange, waving his sabre, cut his way through Wheeler's aides and dashed at the skinny Confederate general, ready to slice him in two, only to have Wheeler escape by jumping a fence with his horse, and a cursing LaGrange's mount refused to follow.

The serenade threaded its way through his thoughts:

"Then cheer upon cheer for bold Sherman,
"Went out through each valley and glen,
"And the bugles re-echoed the music,
"That came from the lips of the men.

"For we knew that the stars in our banner,
"More bright in their splendor would be,
"And that blessings from Northland would greet us,
"While Sherman marched down to the sea."

Atlanta. A great city in flames, a bewildered population
clogging the roads, escaping to nowhere, for there was nowhere to escape. Shouting men, crying women, wailing children and infants. And the darkies by the thousands trailed
behind the army, praising "de jubilo," and singing "God bless
Massa Lincum."

"So forward boys, forward to battle,
"We marched on our wearisome way,
"And we stormed the wild hills at Resaca,
"God bless those who fell on that day."

Yes, God bless them all, blue and gray. The hundreds of
thousands now buried beneath the earth, from the lowliest
private all the way up to the President. Dead now, but not
forgotten.

"And Kenesaw wild in its glory,
"Frowned down on the flag of the free,
"As east and west bore her standard,
"As Sherman marched down to the sea."

He had never been as idealistic as Stannie. He had joined
the war as a lark, with a schoolboy's juvenile enthusiasm.
Stannie had understood, from the very beginning, what it
was all about. Charlie Fay, after all the bloodshed and misery,
still wondered why any of it had happened in the first place,
and what really had been accomplished. He realized he would
never make sense of it all. But Stannie knew. He knew because

he was the better man.

The concert over, Sherman and his aides had applauded the musicians and retired back into the house. The knot of officers and enlisted men who had stopped to listen broke apart, Charlie and Stannie retiring to the campfire outside Charlie's tent and sharing thoughts of home, the war and too much good whiskey.

But that was last night and today Charlie Fay didn't relish the thought of Meriwether Pickens skulking in the woods, maybe lying in ambush for his best friend. There was something more between the two than mutual hatred. He felt it deep inside him. Stannie was keeping something back, a dark secret shared between he and Pickens, and one that would soon come to a violent head. One that Charlie Fay had to try to prevent. He rose from his camp stool and set off down the road in search of Stannie.

When he heard a shot and the confused shouts of the pickets, Fay had a sudden sense of foreboding and rushed toward the commotion. He cut off the road and through a break in the trees into a small clearing, where he saw Stannie lying on his back in the mud, an ugly, bloody hole in the front of his tunic.

"Stannie!" he screamed. "My God!" He raced to his fallen friend and knelt before him. Two pickets were standing over the body.

"Nothin' we kin do, Lieutenant," said one. "Lung shot."

In the woods beyond the clearing, Fay could hear other pickets beating the brush for the suspected rebel sniper. Fay slid his hand under Short's limp body and pulled him close. Short stared at him, wide-eyed. Fay knew the look: It was the fear of death. He had seen it dozens of times on other men as they slowly bled to death from battle wounds. On his friend, however, the look took on a new, more terrible meaning.

"Stannie," said Fay. "Who did this to you? Was it Pickens?"

Short's breath began to come in a rattling wheeze, like a broken-down engine. Fay pulled Short closer to him. "Who, Stannie?" he repeated. "Who?"

The last breath from Stanford Short's lungs expired, and the boy's eyes turned glassy.

Charlie Fay began to cry. He gently lowered Stannie to the damp ground, stood and wiped his eyes with the back of his hand. He saw the faint tracks leading away from the rock outcropping.

"Pickens," he whispered in a snake-like hiss.

He bent into a hunter's crouch and broke into a slow trot, following the tracks out of the clearing and into the woods.

CHAPTER THIRTY-FIVE
1991

Tony O'Connor slapped an angry palm against his forehead. "You again?" he moaned as Moon marched through his office door.

"I made a mistake." Moon wasn't buying O'Connor's B-movie, tough cop act.

"Your *mother* made a mistake," countered O'Connor sourly. "When she had you."

Sticks and stones, thought Moon. "Owen didn't murder Elaine Haskell."

O'Connor shook a cautionary finger. "Don't tell me that, Moon. We know he shot Manny. And as far as the Haskell woman's murder, the evidence points to him. He's upstairs now, locked in a cell. In a few more hours, he'll crack and confess."

"Confess like Mark Kieth?"

O'Connor slammed his fist on his desk. His styrofoam coffee cup leaped up and landed on its side, splashing thick, inky liquid on a short stack of typed sheets. "Goddammit, Moon! One more word ...*one* more, goddammit, and I'll have your ass in the cell next to Owen's upstairs!"

"Oh, knock it off. You're acting like a stereotypical cop in

a crummy detective movie. His mother killed Elaine Haskell,"
Moon continued, inwardly beginning to worry if he had really pushed the stressed-out cop over the edge.

O'Connor shook his thick Irish head in disbelief. "Do
you know who you're accusing? Do you know the kind of
power she has?"

"Yes, I do. Which is why we have to work fast."

"We?"

"Yes, Tony. We can cut Lydia Owen off at the pass. I'm sure
she has her attorney hard at work right now, crafting her alibi,
putting up a paper wall around her."

"And what do you suggest we do?"

"You have a friend in the courts? Better yet, does Lydia
Owen have any enemies in the courts?"

"Judge Terri Malinski is both. Terri hates her dad, and he's
allied with the Owen family."

"Then get Malinski to issue a search warrant for Lydia
Owen's home. I'm positive she's hiding the murder weapon
somewhere on the premises."

"Can you clue me in on what the murder weapon is supposed to be?"

"A ballpeen hammer."

A spark of respect flashed in O'Connor's eyes. "Where
did you get privileged information?"

"I'm a newspaperman, Tony. I have my sources. Are we
going to get that search warrant?"

"Give me one good reason why I should believe you."

"Because you know me, Tony. I may have my faults, but
you know goddam well that when I dig up with information, it's almost always on the money. Besides, if you don't
trust me, maybe Parker will." Crispin Parker, the highest-rank-
ing black cop on the force, was bucking for chief, once gray-
haired and senile Stephen Torrance who had been chief for
nearly twenty years, finally stepped down. Moon knew that

O'Connor (who also wanted the chief's job) couldn't risk Parker making such an important collar. It had been a cheap but necessary shot.

"And Tony," continued Moon, salting the wound. "Parker would make a horseshit chief."

O'Connor looked at Moon with a newly-discovered admiration. "You're a real bastard, aren't you Moon? You know all the right buttons to push."

Moon gave him a congratulatory slap on the back. "I *am* a bastard. And you're a brave man, Tony. And a smart cop. This is going to earn you that promotion."

"Collaring someone like Lydia Owen never earned anyone a promotion, Moon. I can't believe you're talking me into this, but you're right—Parker would make a lousy chief."

✮✮✮

Gripping her open front door, Lydia Owen stared unbelievingly at the search warrant, then glanced over her shoulder as if her conscience was sneaking up on her. Moon noticed a trace of panic in her eyes.

"It's a search warrant, Ma'am," said Tony O'Connor. He was respectful, but not awed by her power and prestige.

"Who signed that warrant?" Lydia Owen demanded. Moon had played this stand-and-wait-at-the-front-door game with her before. It was just as unpleasant the second time around. The tips of his toes were ice-cold. His mustache was beginning to freeze.

"Judge Malinski, Ma'am."

"I'll have to speak to her father about this. He's a very good friend of the family. Do you know him?"

"Walter Malinski? Head of the local Democratic Party? State Senator? I know *of* him, Ma'am, but I don't know him. We move in different social circles." O'Connor sneaked his toe tentatively past the threshold.

Stiffening like she had a steel rod for a spine, the old lady commanded, "Take another step inside this house, and your career is finished, Sergeant."

"It's Captain, Ma'am," said the cop, bristling. He walked inside the home. Moon attempted to follow, but Lydia Owen placed her arm across the doorway, preventing him from entering.

"He's with me, Mrs. Owen," said Tony O'Connor. "But he can't come in unless you invite him."

Recognizing the implicit warning in his voice, Lydia Owen reluctantly let her arm drop and invited Moon inside. "Nice to see you again, Mrs. Owen," said Moon, stepping past her.

"My attorney will be here shortly, Captain ..."

"O'Connor, Ma'am. Tony O'Connor." The cop stared at his opulent surroundings, puckered his lips and whistled. "You'll forgive me, Mrs. Owen, but most of the people we deal with are on the lower end of the social strata. I knew places like this existed, but ..." He shook his head in silent admiration.

Impatiently, Lydia Owen said, "You have a search warrant, Captain. I assume you're here to search for something. If you'd tell me what it is, perhaps I can assist you." Moon noticed that a single strand of her helmet-like hair had come undone, winding like a silver serpent down her forehead.

"A ballpeen hammer, Mrs. Owen," offered Moon. "The one you used to murder Elaine Haskell."

"As I told you yesterday, that is a preposterous and libelous accusation, young man," replied Lydia Owen, watching nervously as Tony O'Connor moved through the foyer and toward the rear of the home. Moon heard him open a door, take a few steps and then open another door and descend into what Moon supposed was the basement. As Lydia Owen babbled on about her attorneys, Moon tilted his head, straining to hear O'Connor's footsteps below; there was a rattling of what sounded like metal against wood, then a pause. After a moment, he heard the footsteps again as O'Connor mounted the steps and worked his way through the house and back to the foyer.

"And furthermore," Lydia Owen was lecturing Moon when O'Connor came back into view, holding a ballpeen hammer gingerly by the tip of the handle between thumb and forefinger. Moon saw the cop had pushed his hair behind his ears. He had never really noticed O'Connor's ears before. They were tiny and stood out at the sides of his head, like little monkey's ears.

The cop was smiling broadly. "Always look in the basement, where the old man keeps his tools. Look at this," he said, holding the hammer up for Moon to see. "And it's even got blood on the head."

Open-mouthed, a chagrined Lydia Owen sucked in her breath. Her steely demeanor broke like a mud-walled dam at flood tide. Her hair popped like loose springs, her arms flopped loosely at her sides, her head swayed like it was on ball bearings and her knees became jelly as Lydia Owen rolled her eyes toward the ceiling and collapsed onto the floor.

"Jesus H. Christ!" Holding the hammer, O'Connor raced to the prostrate woman as Moon knelt and ineffectually patted her wrist like Lew Ayers in an old *Doctor Kildare* movie.

✯✯✯

Leaving O'Connor, and a revived but shamed and distraught Lydia Owen, Moon drove back to his apartment. The thought of the Sherman letter in his dresser drawer gave him cold sweats. Three people had already died because of it, and he didn't plan on being the fourth. Tessie Allen had mentioned a curse when referring to the Stanford Short letters. It seemed melodramatic at the time but it rang true now. Moon climbed the stairs to his room, opened his dresser drawer and checked for the letter, half hoping it had disappeared during the night. He'd thought about giving it to Karl or Hippo, or maybe showing it to Sally. As far as he knew, he was the only living person who knew of the existence of the Sherman letter, outside of Harold Owen, and Owen couldn't prove he'd seen the original. Karl had also seen only the copy.

Too exhausted to think about the letter any more, he pulled his Murphy bed out of the wall and collapsed onto the sagging mattress and squeaking springs. He dreamed about his pa when he was sick in his hospital bed. General Sherman was in the bed next to his, and the two of them were playing chess on a table between them. Moon's father was winning, and the General was getting mad. Outside the hospital windows, B-52s were dropping ordnance on Civil War troops, who were being tossed in the air like rag dolls, torn into bits and pieces. A group of '60s antiwar protesters were marching in front of the soldiers, carrying "Get Out of the South" placards and singing Give Peace a Chance. Moon and Sally were standing naked in the hospital room, watching Moon's father whip General Sherman at chess. Moon's mother was sitting at a table in the corner of the room, frizzy hair bound in curlers, dressed in a wrinkled nightgown and fuzzy slippers. She was hunched over a cup of black coffee, baggy-eyed, counting her nine-ball winnings from the night before.

Moon supposed he'd had more bizarre dreams, but he couldn't remember when.

CHAPTER THIRTY-SIX

Moon drove north on Sheridan Road and turned into the Saint Ignatious campus. The picture-postcard college was blanketed in pristine snow, with the meandering Bass River dividing the campus, the main buildings perched on high bluffs facing Lake Michigan. He crossed a red, arched bridge over the frozen river and parked in a lot in front of the Administration Building.

Karl Von Essen's office was little more than a closet with a desk and chair. Karl sat at the desk, behind a messy stack of student papers and books. He was bewildered by Moon's statement that he hadn't been able to locate the original of the Sherman letter.

"Couldn't you still publish research on the letter, using the copy I gave you?" said Moon. He could see Sally chiding him that Karl Von Essen wasn't his responsibility, either. But Karl was Hippo's brother-in-law. Hippo had asked Moon to give Karl a chance to work on the letters, to help the man secure tenure at the college, and Moon had come to try to settle the debt.

"Certainly not," Karl replied, crestfallen. "If I were to do that, without being able to substantiate that the letter had once existed, I'd be laughed out of the research community. Damn! I've got to find that letter if it takes forever!" Books and papers leaped as he slammed his fist down upon the desk.

"I'd think twice about that. I wouldn't want you to go off on a wild-goose chase." Moon had created a Lost Dutchman mine for Karl, but he hadn't given him a map—or a pick and shovel. Karl had become another victim of the Sherman letter. Moon hoped it wouldn't drive him to drink or cost him his family. He knew nothing in the world was worth that sacrifice.

Climbing back into the Rambler and driving off campus, Moon reflected on his powerful urge to have a drink—any kind of drink—just as long as it allowed him to surrender to sweet oblivion. It seemed life was once again beginning to overwhelm him, as it had when his marriage began to implode and he realized as he slid into bed beside his wife that he actually *hated* this woman; hated to look at her, to touch her, to force a smile and peck at her proffered (and despised) cheek at public gatherings; and the ego-shattering realization that his wife hated him as well and also wanted to make an end of their sham marriage.

The girls—that had been the hard part. The oldest, Laura, had wailed as he packed his bags and exited out the front door, his life's possessions stuffed into two battered leather suitcases. Her two sisters had hung onto their mother's skirts (Marie, the youngest, sucking her thumb in bewilderment) while Marsha affected a self-righteous pose: the abused wife casting her spouse from her home. He had wanted to sneak out in the night, to spare his daughters the pain of having to watch him leave—probably forever—but Marsha (the witch) had denied him access to the house until all three girls had arrived home from school and he was forced to undergo the pain and humiliation of being kicked out of *his* house; the home he had busted his ass to purchase and maintain; the too-expensive home he had never really wanted with its over-priced furnishings and smarmy prints on the wall—pedantic trappings demanded by his social-climber wife to impress the crowd of local movers and shakers she so desperately wanted to join, rubbing shoulders with emotional and spiritual cripples for whom life meant nothing more than a bigger house, a newer car and a vacation to ever distant (and more exclusive) never-never lands.

Now he fought the burning desire to drink, forcing himself instead to think of his daughters, and the futile hopelessness in Karl Von Essen's red-rimmed eyes. He passed a tavern (bright red neon Bud sign blinking in the window) and the Rambler turned into the parking lot as if it had a mind of its own. He sat, trembling hands clutching the steering wheel, engine idling. To surrender now, to enter the deep, dark womb of the tavern and order up a shot and beer would mean to admit defeat, to quit before the job was finished.

There was more to do, so much more to do.

He courageously put the Rambler in reverse, slowly backed out of the tavern parking lot and drove back to his cramped apartment and blissful, sober sleep.

CHAPTER THIRTY-SEVEN

1865

Pickens ran for over a mile before collapsing at the foot of a huge rotted stump. Gasping for air, he dragged himself up, leaned against the spongy wood. The rifle at his feet lay like a dead thing—inanimate wood and iron. He began to giggle; a nervous wheeze at first, then a high-pitched squeak and finally a demonic bellow.

"Short!" he whooped. "I kilt you, you high-handed sumbitch! I kilt you!" He danced a pagan jig until breathless, hands on his hips, he tilted his chin skyward and howled.

Spent, he leaned back against the stump. "What's 'at?" he suddenly whispered, jerking his head toward the sound of something moving toward him in the brush.

★★★

Broken branches, deep prints in the soft spring earth, a piece of tattered blue uniform hanging off a thorny bush ... Pickens had stumbled through the woods like a drunken sailor on shore leave, pointing the way for a murderous Charlie Fay bent on revenge.

Fay, alerted by Pickens' whooping, swiftly moved through the thick underbrush toward the sound. Hate coursed like an electric current through his veins. Ahead was the vermin who had executed his best friend and in Charlie Fay's opinion the finest man who had ever lived. Stannie had survived four years of terrible war, only to be shot like a dog by a piece of human filth who did not deserve the gift of life.

Fay was a menacing cauldron of rage. He unholstered his pistol as he spotted Pickens' frenzied silhouette through the tangle of leaves.

★★★

Pickens scurried behind the shelter of the stump, ready to ambush the threatening presence moving swiftly toward him from the wood. He reached for his rifle and gasped. The rifle! He had left it on the other side of the stump. A mere few feet away, it might as well have been ten miles. Not wishing to expose himself, but having no other recourse, he made his move. On hands and knees, he slithered around the trunk's ten foot circumference and reached for the rifle barrel.

"Hold it there, Pickens." Pickens froze and looked up to see Charlie Fay, his Navy Colt leveled on Pickens' worthless heart.

"Drop the rifle," Fay commanded. Pickens meekly let go of the weapon.

Fay motioned with the pistol. "Now stand up, Pickens."

Pickens realized he was in mortal danger. "What's th' matter Charlie?" he whined as he stood. "Why you holdin' that pistol on me? I ain't done nothin'! Everythin' always happens t' me!"

Fay curled his lip in disgust at Pickens' obsequiousness. He and Stannie should have run the man out of Camp Henry on a rail, four years ago, before the hard campaigning. If they had done that, Stannie would still be alive. Stannie ... for a fleeting moment, the image of his good and noble friend flashed before Charlie Fay's eyes. He aimed the pistol at Pickens' head, his finger wrapped around the trigger. "Don't die with a lie on your lips, Pickens. Why did you kill Stannie?"

Pickens dropped to his knees and clasped his hands in supplication. "Please Lieutenant," he begged. "I didn't mean to. It was me or him. He wanted the letter. I wouldn't give it to him."

"What letter?" Fay felt the absolute power behind his pistol, but he did not revel in it. This would be justice in its most elemental form —an eye for an eye. No more, no less.

Pickens replied in a sycophantic snivel. "Why, the letter the gen'ral writ. If it got published, it would go bad fer th' gen'ral. Th' cap'n wanted to publish it fer th' money. I wouldn't let him do it."

"I don't know what letter you're talking about, Pickens. I warned you not to die with a lie on your lips. Stannie would never jeopardize his commanding officer's reputation. Certainly not for money."

"Now lieutenant." Pickens attempted a conciliatory smile, revealing his rotted teeth. "Don't be too hasty. If'n we kin git that letter, you an' me could make some real money. Whaddyou say?" His jaundiced eyes skittered to and fro in their sockets, avoiding Fay's uncompromising stare.

"I say this, Pickens." Fay squeezed his finger tighter on the trigger. Pickens squealed, curling his arms around his head, kneeling in a fetal crouch. Charlie Fay hesitated. He had killed Rebs during the war, but they were the enemy. This was different. But he couldn't leave Pickens to military justice. There were no witnesses to Stannie's murder, and Pickens in all likelihood would go free. He swallowed and steeled himself for what he knew he must deliver ...justice for Stanford Short.

Fay took a deep breath. "Like killing a dog," he mumbled, taking aim and pulling the trigger. Pickens squealed again as the Colt barked and blasted a bloody hole into his brown, greasy curls.

Charlie Fay holstered the pistol and turned back the way he had come, never looking back at Pickens' body. Pickens would soon be food for the crows and the foxes and then his bleached bones would sink into the earth, like the bones of the thousands who had preceded him. Another nameless casualty in an endless war.

Yet one thing nagged at him ... what did Pickens mean by "the letter the general wrote?" Had Stannie died for nothing more than a piece of paper to satisfy the greed of an evil ne'er-do-well? Head between his hands, he whispered, "No more. No more." He put the thought behind him forever.

He hungered to see Elaine, to sit by a fireplace with books and pipe in his home while Elaine's fingers danced across the piano, filling the room with sweet music. He wanted to see his children, laughing by the firelight. Later, in the still of night, he would snuggle up to Elaine, his wife, in his bed and share with her the secret pleasures God and good fortune had reserved for them. And by God, it would happen! His enlistment would be up soon, and when it was he would go back home. He would burn his uniform and bury his pistol and saber and never again take up arms against any man.

Charlie Fay breathed deep the fresh spring air. The war was finally over. "God rest you, Stanford Short," he said. "I'm going home."

CHAPTER THIRTY-EIGHT

1991

"I haven't been much help, I'm afraid," said Hippo as he dug a sensuously-carved brier wood pipe into a pouch of Bugler tobacco. In front of him sat an empty plate, except for a solitary French fry—the sole survivor of his lake perch, cole slaw and fries.

"Where's your playmate?" Moon asked, looking around for Dean Paskewicz.

"I gave him the day off," said the bookie. Behind him on the restaurant wall was a big travel poster of a bright tropical beach dotted with palm trees. Moon wondered if Sally would like to fly down to the Bahamas on her next vacation. They could lounge on the beach, drink Pina Coladas, snorkel, maybe make love in the sand, surf pounding over them, like Burt Lancaster and Deborah Kerr in From Here to Eternity. It could revive their tenuous relationship.

"Did you hear me, Moon?" Hippo said.

"I'm sorry, Hippo. What did you say?"

"I said that I'm afraid I haven't been much help to you in this whole affair. You seem to have done everything yourself."

"If you hadn't sent me over to Karl, Mark Keith's name never would've been cleared."

"It'll never truly be cleared. And to be brutally honest,

nobody gives a shit. The guy was a bum."

"I'm shocked, Hippo. The man was innocent. It was our duty to see it through to the end."

"Our duty? For a Chicago saloon brat, Moon, you amaze me. The issue of crime and punishment is a lot more complicated than most people realize."

"I'm not an attorney."

"That's evident. You'd make a terrible attorney. Underneath that rough exterior hides an unabashed idealist. It's why you're such a lousy gambler. You bet from the heart, Moon. It makes you an easy mark."

"What makes you think I'm such an idealist?"

"Who'd waste his hard-earned money and vacation defending a man like Mark Keith but a starry-eyed idealist? And who would put the time and effort into defending another man he believes is a prisoner of circumstances, a man he dislikes intensely?"

"What're you driving at?"

"I think you know—Harold Owen. You believe he's an innocent victim, don't you? Didn't he also tell you that he's bereft of funds and that his mother refuses to pay for his defense?"

How in the hell did Hippo know that, thought Moon. "'Bereft of funds.' Only you can put it that way, Hippo."

"You do agree with me, then? You plan to work on Harold Owens' behalf?"

"I wanted that bastard, Hippo. I wanted him so bad I could taste it. I thought I had him, too."

"And now you're going to assist in his defense against the Manny Edison murder charge."

"I've—we've—already scored a neat coup, getting Lydia Owen indicted for Elaine Haskell's' murder."

"For an amateur, it was a nice bit of detective work, tying her in with the hammer. Where did you say it came from again?"

"In her husband's basement workshop. He was a million-aire, but he was still a tinkerer at heart. We found the ball-peen hammer hanging there with bits of blood on it that matched Elaine Haskell's blood type. Lydia Owen hadn't even bothered to hide the evidence. It didn't take much work after that to link her to the murder. They matched her prints against prints they found in Haskell's home, plus some fibers from her clothing. When she was confronted with the facts, she collapsed and confessed. I enjoyed watching that old witch crack."

"In the long run, Moon, it was a stupid move. Involving yourself in a criminal investigation in which you had no personal stake."

"My reward was a great story. Any reporter would kill for it."

The gambler shrugged. "If you want to believe that, fine. Now tell me, are you going to work on his defense?"

"What is this, a cross-examination?"

"Are you?" He leaned forward, poking with his pipe aggressively.

"Yes," Moon conceded. "I am."

Hippo jabbed the pipe between clenched teeth. "Good," he said. "I'm no starry-eyed idealist, but the man who bumped off Manny Edison deserves more than moral support. I'll call in some markers on a certain very capable local attorney. He'll take the case pro bono. And I'm sure I can find a sympathetic judge to hear the case—just to piss off the cops."

Moon laughed so hard that he thought he saw the palm fronds tremble on the poster.

CHAPTER THIRTY-NINE

Thousands of pages have been written about the beauty and grandeur of Lake Michigan, but in Moon's book the lake was most spectacular under a full moon in winter.

He sat with the bruised but unbowed Sally Andrews in a park overlooking the lake, under just such a moon. The Rambler's engine was running, and its wheezing heater was going full blast. They gazed down over the sloping bluffs to the beach below, covered in sculptured snow drifts. The lakeshore was encrusted as high as fifteen feet with thick ice, and farther out ice floes reflected glowing moonlight.

"When we were kids, we called going down to the lake to park and neck 'watching the submarine races,'" said Sally.

"That's creative. Didn't know you Wisconsin folks had it in you." He could feel the warmth of her thin body, the rounded edge of her shoulder lightly touching his chest.

"I hope you're not going to pull that old 'cheesehead' line on me Moon." Sally gazed out over the moonlit ice floes and said, "It's magnificent, isn't it?"

"I guess."

"What's the matter? You seem down."

"It just occurred to me that I squandered my entire vacation, and never saw my daughters once. In fact, I barely thought about them."

"You can make it up to them, Moon."

"It bothers me. It really does."

"Do you ever miss them enough to try to get back together with Marsha?"

"Never. Don't get me wrong, I miss them terribly, but a little bit of Marsha goes a long way. She was more worried about her career than our marriage."

"I'd watch it with that talk, Moon. Keep them barefoot and pregnant, huh?"

"Not at all, Sally. Everything in the home was in second place to Marsha. Me. The kids. It just made it hard, that's all. And I wasn't exactly the model husband, either."

"Her career really seems in high gear now: Head of the Department of Social Services."

"Yup. She can read a computer print-out with the best of them. And do lunch—let's not forget that."

"Bitter words."

"I won't try to hide the fact. I couldn't live in the world she wanted: pressing the flesh; laughing at unfunny jokes; kissing ass to get ahead. That's why I like what I'm doing now. I can write whatever I want—within limits—and then get up from my desk and leave it all there."

"Sort of the lone wolf of the newspaper industry?"

"I guess you could call me that. It comes with a minimum of strings attached. As long as I know where I stand on facts and figures and stay at arm's length from libel, I'm pretty much on my own. They don't pay much at The Express, but I get a long leash, and I'll settle for that."

"What do you want, Moon?"

"Me? I want milk to come in glass bottles, with a paper top I can lick the cream off, delivered to the front porch by a milkman. I want to see the return of double features and gas jockeys in uniform who'll wipe down your windshield and check the air in your tires. I want to see a heavyweight boxing champ with class, like Joe Louis or Rocky Marciano. I want to see real give and take on the screen, like Tracy and Hepburn, and a genuine, Gable-and-Lombard Hollywood romance that can't be smeared by supermarket tabloids. And once before I die, I want to see the Cubs in the World Series."

She laughed. "You really don't belong, do you, Moon? You're out of touch, like your old movies."

"You'd prefer me as a member of the suit-and-tie crowd, the 'Now' Generation?"

"I didn't say that. I wouldn't want to see you any other way."

"So what are you saying, Sally?" Like a boxer caught flat-footed, he could see it coming: a long roundhouse right he was powerless to stop.

"I'm saying that I think we've been seeing too much of each other." Her tone was clipped and matter-of-fact. She didn't want to hurt him any more than she had to.

"Uh huh."

"And that Frank Koslowski is coming over tonight for dinner and I've got to get home ASAP."

"Frank Koslowski?" Moon couldn't stand the overly hand-some butt-kisser who was first in line for the next *Southport Times* editorship. Perfect managerial material: an asshole.

"Marry me, Sally."

"You're dangerous, Moon. A windmill chaser. Don Quixote."

"Then be my Dulcinea."

"Moon," she said sadly. "You're so full of crap. Take me home."

She leaned over and kissed him—a long, sad, goodbye kiss.

CHAPTER FORTY

====================

Midnight.

Moon unwrapped a Milky Way and bit down, the rich chocolate melting in his mouth and sweet caramel sticking to his molars. He wasn't getting any younger. He'd have to get off these candy bars—or at least cut back—and start eating more real food.

He'd just finished watching a rented videotape and he wasn't happy. Max Nussbaum, owner of Max's Video Paradise, had forced on him *The Haunting* with Julie Harris, and like the other three times he'd seen it, it had scared the shit out of him. Moon believed it was easily the most frightening movie ever made—even more than *The Cabinet of Doctor Caligari*, the silent vampire classic. No blood. No guts. No slashers carving up scantily-clad teenage nymphets. Just profound psychological horror, where your own mind created your own monsters.

"Max, you SOB," Moon said as he hit the VCR on rewind. The TV instantly popped back on, tuned to CNN. An interviewer was questioning three psychologists about Saddam Hussein. One of them, a chunky woman with unruly hair, said that Hussein was the classic megalomaniac. "He will go down in flames," she said, "dragging his country with him. He wants to be a martyr."

"Great," Moon said to the screen. "Just dandy." Bathed in the TV's blue light, he leaned back in his chair, muted the TV with the remote, and opened the copy of the Stanford Short obituary Tessie Allen had given him at the Historical Society those few long days ago. He read slowly, silently mouthing the words:

Death of Capt. Stanford Short
(of the 1st Wis Cavalry)

E.M. Kinney Esq has received the following letter giving account of the death of Capt. Short, Co I 1st Wis Cavalry:

> Camp of the 1st Wis. Cavalry
> Before Raleigh N.C.
> April 29 1865
>
> E.M. KINNEY.
> Dear sir:
> Through the circumstances of war, it becomes my sorrowing duty to inform you of the death of Stanford M. Short, Capt Co I 1st Wis. Cavalry.
> He was shot April 29 by one of the enemy's sharp shooters, most tragically, after the peace terms with General Johnston had been signed and all thought the area about had been quit of enemy activity.
> The shot took effect just below the collar bone of the right shoulder, hit the right lung; cut the windpipe, and lodged in the left side of the neck.
> He lived about 20 minutes but could not speak after he was hit.
> We feel that we have met with a great loss—While we who knew him only as an agreeable associate, a warm-hearted friend,

*and a generous commander and lament his early departure, we can
but think of the sorrow and grief that will fill the hearts of those
who knew him by the dearer ties of brother, and son.*

*The loss comes so heavily upon me that I know not what to
say.*

He was esteemed by officers and men of the regiment.

Yours Respectfully.
Charles L. Fay Lieut,
Co I 1st Wis Cavalry

Moon brushed a tear from his eye. Not only for the long-
dead Stanford Short, but for Elaine Haskell, Mark Keith and
Tessie Allen as well, who had died as an indirect result of this
boy's actions 126 years before.

"We're kindred spirits, I think, Stanford Short." Moon
went to the bentwood coat rack near his apartment door, took
the Sherman letter out of his coat pocket and took it back to
his chair to reread. It was obvious Short had stolen the letter,
but why? He had taken a tremendous chance in doing so, but
he had probably stolen it out of a moral obligation to both
his country and his general. If Stanton had gotten hold of the
letter, it would have been the final nail in Sherman's coffin,
ending a glorious career in disgrace and probably a hangman's
noose. Moon slid the letter back into the envelope. Karl Von
Essen was right about one thing: The boy had been a hero of
the highest order. And no one would ever know. Stanford
Short hadn't wanted anyone to see the letter, to sully his
general's reputation, to destroy the Union. They never would.

Moon reached into his pocket and pulled out a matchbook
that read: "DiCiccio's Bar & Grill. In God we trust. All others
pay cash." His hand was shaking. He tore out a match and
struck it on the cover strip. The flame leaped up in a tiny puff
of smoke—blue, yellow, orange. He held it out in one hand,

the envelope in the other, until the flame almost reached his thumb and forefinger. Then he moved the match under the corner of the envelope and watched fire engulf it and the letter inside.

Moon walked the burning paper to his kitchen and dropped it in the sink. The fire consumed it hungrily, leaving a wrinkled pile of black ash. He turned on the faucet and washed it all down the drain, leaving nothing but a slight acrid smell. He had just incinerated a million bucks, but somehow he felt curiously fulfilled.

Moon stretched out on his Murphy bed, his feet draped over the edge. The psychologists were still mutely arguing on the television. How would all this Gulf craziness shake out in a 100 years? He decided not to worry about it. Better to leave the forces of history alone.

Moon closed his eyes and fell asleep.

Notes on THE SHERMAN LETTER

Could Sherman have written such a letter? He was known as a brilliant, ruthless and impetuous man who had no patience for fools. And as to the circumstances surrounding the time the letter in the novel was written, Sherman mentions in his memoirs that he had been "not only angry," (with Stanton's published remarks) "I was outraged, and determined to set things right." Perfect material for an historic conceit.

Most of the Stanford Short letters in the novel are taken from the collected letters of Willie Shepherd, a Kenosha, Wisconsin, boy who served in the Civil War and who local scholars believe may have read General Grant's mail. With the exception of a few published in local papers during the war, none has ever seen publication. The description of Lincoln in the Short letters is taken from a letter written by Cordelia Harvey, another Kenoshan, who was a pivotal figure in the hospital services during the conflict and who met Mr. Lincoln on several occasions. Stanford Short's obituary was taken nearly verbatim from the *Southport Telegraph*, and is the obituary of Captain William Stetson of Kenosha, who was killed by a sniper's bullet at Spanish Fort, Alabama on April 2, 1865, a week before Lee surrendered to Grant.

Written permission has been granted by the Kenosha County Historical Society to use these historic treasures in the novel. The Sherman letter, of course, is a fabrication.

A huge thank you to Kenosha County Historical Society Executive Director Dane Pollei, who gave me the initial go-ahead to use the Shepherd letters and who read the novel in its infancy and gave me much encouragement along the way.

And a final thanks goes out to historian Henry LaMont, who assisted me in tracing the movements of the 1st Wisconsin Cavalry and General Sherman during the waning days of the war.